Afta-U

D.J. Winston

JENNIFER-LYNN KENISTON

TATE PUBLISHING
AND ENTERPRISES, LLC

Published by Tate Publishing & Enterprises, LLC
127 E. Trade Center Terrace | Mustang, Oklahoma 73064 USA
1.888.361.9473 | www.tatepublishing.com

Tate Publishing is committed to excellence in the publishing industry. The company reflects the philosophy established by the founders, based on Psalm 68:11,
"The Lord gave the word and great was the company of those who published it."

Book design copyright © 2015 by Tate Publishing, LLC. All rights reserved.
Edition 1, Second Issue.
Edited by Mike Ball
Cover design by Ivan Charlem Igot
Interior design by Gram Telen
Cover drawing of the Afta-U boat by Christina Dell

Published in the United States of America
ISBN: 978-1-68028-427-0
Fiction / Thrillers / Crime
15.10.20

To my mother, Judith-Lynn Keniston, who has always encouraged me to pursue my dreams and the creative writing soul inside of me.

In loving memory of my two biggest supporters smiling down from heaven, my father, Ronald Keniston, and my grandmother, Jean Harrison.

Acknowledgments

This book is near and dear to me, and it could only have been be completed with God's grace and guidance. Most people name a book somewhere during the process of writing it, but I started this one with the title and a single paragraph. The title was personal; *Afta-U* was the name of the Flying Scot sailboat owned by my maternal grandfather, Norman Harrison. Over a period of years, I wrote this novel out of order, then worked to bring it all together.

First and foremost, I want to express my appreciation and gratitude to my editor, Mike Ball, who jumped in at the eleventh hour, and somehow worked alongside me to polish and perfect every sentence in this story to make it what is today.

I also want to extend a special heartfelt thank-you to Linzi Strong, Lisa Schneider, and JoAnn Fitts for providing immeasurable hours of encouragement and feedback. To all my other friends and family who supported me on this journey, I thank you from the bottom of my heart.

I am reminded of a lesson I learned from my life coach, Edward Langan; "Like the road to Hana, it's about the journey, not the destination."

What a blessed and wonderful journey this has been.

Afta-U

The vessel sailed
Anticipating calmness
Overturned by Fate

Chapter I

The brown paper grocery bag ripped open, setting free my cardboard carton of eggs, so that they tumbled out in a slow, lazy arc and landed on the kitchen floor. Five out of the twelve eggs broke or cracked open in a chaotic mess on the tiles below, a slimy testament to my attempt to juggle everything in from the car in one trip. As I crouched down to clean up the mess, the pain shooting down my back reminded me that I was nearly forty years old.

I wanted to laugh, and I wanted to cry.

As I dropped the paper towel loaded with egg glop and shells into the trash bin, I thought about something I'd read once: when an egg is cracked open from the outside, whatever is inside dies. But when the egg is cracked open from the inside, it yields life.

So here I was, the baby chick waiting to break out of my shell, while the outside world was slowly and relentlessly pushing back in on me and forming a terrifying web of surface cracks. I knew that I would eventually break through that shell, but I had no idea whether my personal barrier would crack open from the inside, setting me free, or crash in from the outside and crush the life out of me.

Then it dawned on me that even though life may survive long enough to make it out of the shell, all new life is fragile and vulnerable.

Throughout the years, I've found that certain works of literature and poetry have held up a mirror to my life. One of the most notable is the conclusion of one of Stevie Smith's poems: "I was much too far out all my life/And not waving but drowning."

Then there is the final sentence from F. Scott Fitzgerald's *The Great Gatsby*: "So we beat on, boats against the current, borne back ceaselessly into the past." I knew that I was trapped in a past that I just couldn't escape, and I often felt as if I were drowning in the powerful current of my life.

It seems like that current has always pulled me back to you, my childhood best friend, Hope Marksman. Constant reminders of you swirled around me every day. I could hear your laugh in the physical walls of my current house and in the land itself, haunting echoes of my childhood memories of you.

One of my most prized investments was a boat named *Afta-U*, which proudly sat on this land.

This boat has tried to keep me afloat, both literally and figuratively, so it was only fitting that I had to find a way to name it after you. Most people name their boats after loved ones, to somehow pass on a form of immortality. Since I couldn't bring myself to say your name out loud, how could I be expected to grant you life and engrave it permanently upon my ship's bow? Only God and I knew the true answer to the frequently posed question about the meaning of the *"U"* in that seemingly playful boat name.

Shortly after we moored the boat in the dry harbor of our yard, my daughter, Margaret, asked me if the boat was named after her. I smiled and replied, "Yes, the boat was named *Afta-U*."

"I knew it!" Meg giggled. I always have to laugh whenever she takes proud credit for that name, but I have never once corrected her.

My husband, Nick, wanted to place the *Afta-U* in front of the large oak tree, but instead we cleared space to the left of it, near the property line with the neighbor's house. The placement and view of the *Afta-U* creates a definitive, invisible boundary that acts like the moat of a medieval castle, tauntingly separating my childhood home from my now more regal adult residence.

How fitting the *Afta-U* rests on this particular lot of land that had once been your family's land. The *Afta-U*'s presence, along with the great oak tree, both act as memorials to remind me daily that you, Hope, once existed in my life.

In contrast to the large oak tree that stands as a memorial to your death, the *Afta-U* is a magnificent vessel that glorifies your life.

After my first novel was published six years ago, I purchased this wooden, 22' 1938 Harrison Butler Z-4 Tonner boat, and had it shipped from England to Massachusetts. Since then, I'd taken loving care to ensure that her initial breathtaking beauty could withstand even the roughest of waters. Even though I worked on small restorations over the past few years, she has remained here in this yard, never touching water other than when heaven's tears flowed from the darkened clouds above.

The Harrison Butler boat was very different from the boat I learned to sail on, my grandfather's 1965 Flying Scot racing sailboat. The *Afta-U* had a long keel, with a lovely heart-shaped transom stern planked in yellow pine copper fastened to steam-bent oak timbers. Thanks to the previous owner, it had a relatively new engine. In the cabin there was a two-burner gas stove and a small stainless steel sink, with a gorgeous antique hand pump. Two twin beds or benches were positioned across from one another, and it contained a functional toilet.

To make sure I captured your purity, I painted her white. When the large white cloth sail was opened, it felt like it could reach the clouds high in the sky, and I felt closer to you. When it was furled, this cloth sail was carefully rolled up and stored in a red protective cover.

Perhaps I should've listened to my husband and docked the *Afta-U* between the house and the oak tree, to block it from my view. Instead, this other haunting memorial was visible to me daily through the kitchen window over the sink.

Over the years, the oak tree has grown so large that it now nearly overpowers the house. I've often stood at the kitchen sink, staring out at it, feeling that it was actually staring me down. It looked darkly ominous standing there alone in the middle of the lawn, untouched by other trees and leaning ever so slightly in the direction of the house. For years now, even the birds have avoided perching and nesting in this tree.

When the wind whips through its leaves, I could've sworn that on more than one occasion I heard the quiet mourning from all those affected by your death.

I guess it's an oxymoron of sorts to be quiet and mourning, yet this was the case in Graytown, Massachusetts. In our tiny rural town everyone whispered gossip, discussing everything imaginable – except your death.

I finished cleaning up the mess from the kitchen floor and put away the remaining groceries. With a newly poured cup of coffee and the town paper in hand, I moved to sit at the large circular brown table in the kitchen. I took a deep breath and blew it out as I started reading the article on the front page.

When I was about halfway done with the article, I chuckled with disgust. "Can you believe these ducks made the front page? They tied up traffic for a half hour crossing the road. Front page!" Then I laughed and asked, "Would you like some coffee in your milk?"

Then I realized that I was holding a conversation with the ghost of an eleven-year-old child who had been dead for twenty-nine years. That cup of freshly brewed black coffee no longer appealed to me, but a splash of color reflected in the large mug drew my eyes back to the dark bark of that tree.

After all of these years, it seemed as if the oak tree finally had a visitor. I thought I could see in those branches the dark blue feathers and white and black speckled face of my deceased childhood parakeet, Tinkerbell. As I stared at the ghostly bird, a suppressed memory from long before your death whirled around in my mind as the wind picked up and moved the branch in the grip of Tinkerbell's spectral claws.

I was seven years old, standing in the den and staring at what appeared to be Tinkerbell's empty cage. I leapt on top of the brown faux leather chair to get a better look. My heart sank when I saw Tinkerbell lying on the bottom of the cage, gasping for breath. All the food was gone, and the water in the container was probably stagnant. It was obvious that the bottom of the cage hadn't been cleaned for some time. I was completely overwhelmed with guilt as I realized that my bird was starving to death from my neglect.

My parents had always given her some water and food when I'd ignored their reminders, but they must have lost track somehow. I knew that my parents weren't to blame; the burden belonged solely on my shoulders. When my aunt had given her as a present for my seventh birthday, I had pleaded, begged, and promised to take full responsibility and care for this bird. My parents felt that I was much too young to take on such a big responsibility, but they had finally given in.

When she heard my sobs from the den, my mother rushed in and stood next to me. She grabbed the cage and rushed to the kitchen. We worked together, trying to hand feed the bird dying of starvation on the bottom of the dirty and neglected cage, but to no avail.

In this moment, I knew that more than your death weighed heavily on my shoulders, and that some loss of innocence occurred before your death. Maybe I deserved to have Tinkerbell's ghostly image haunt me from the oak tree, just as you have relentlessly haunted me from the kitchen chair.

Out of the corner of my eye, I saw Nick emerge from the doorway leading to the garage. I hadn't heard the car pull into the driveway.

As our eyes met, I smiled. Not only did Nick return the smile, but he also tenderly reached down to meet me with his six-foot frame, and ever so gently brushed my lips with a kiss. I kissed him back and decided to try to appreciate what I had in life, rather than obsessing about what I no longer had.

My husband was handsome, and age had only enhanced his distinguished good looks. His full head of light brown hair had only recently received a few gray uninvited guests, and I still loved those piercing blue eyes with extra-long eyelashes that had grabbed my attention almost twenty years ago. Pulling away from the kiss, Nick's smile broadened and his one single dimple took center stage.

"Your turn next time," he said.

"Next time?" I asked.

Our daughter Meg appeared around the corner.

"So how did it go? Should I take our cars off the road now or later?" I questioned.

With distress in her voice Meg said, "Mom, I couldn't parallel park, and I have to re-take the stupid exam. And it sucked when your parking brake didn't work, but the guy let Dad off easy with that one!" She walked over to the medicine drawer and began rummaging through all of the pill bottles. "Where's some Tylenol or aspirin or something? God! I have a migraine starting!"

"Aw honey, I'm sorry. I know how upset you must be," I expressed.

"Upset? Lisa, Michelle, and Tricia all have their licenses! I don't know how I'm going to even show my face at school tomorrow. It's so unfair!" Meg declared.

I pushed myself away from the kitchen table and walked over to grab my purse. Inside, I found a bottle of Tylenol, took out two pills, and placed the bottle on the counter.

"You're a life saver, Mom, thanks," Meg said.

"Not so fast," I said, reaching into the drawer, taking out a knife, and cutting each tablet in half.

"Why do you insist on cutting them up each time?" whined Meg. "I have no problem swallowing them. That's your issue, not mine."

"Meg, you'd better find an attitude adjustment soon because you're starting to give me a headache," I snapped back.

"Oh, loves of my life, please stop the bickering," Nick said as he walked over to pull both of us toward him for a hug. He gently kissed Meg, then me, on the top of our heads.

The hug made me smile, but Meg said, "God, I'm not a baby!" and wiggled out of the embrace.

I smiled up at Nick and dumped two more pills out of the Tylenol container. I handed these to Meg, and drew her a glass of water. I swallowed the original cut-up pills myself.

"Way to make your point, Mom! You're ridiculous sometimes!" Meg shouted as she left the room.

I sighed and turned back to my husband. "Any for you? Or can I offer you something stronger – like maybe a shot of Jäger?"

"Cute, Jean, cute," Nick replied.

My daughter was right; it was my issue and not hers. I knew the roots of my issue ran far deeper than the need to cut up pills.

Later that night I found myself standing in the center of the bedroom gagging and choking, trying to spit out phantom pills I believed were lodged in my throat. Nick was standing next to me, trying to wake me up gently. "Honey, it's all right. Jean, wake up. You're all right now."

I muttered a soft "thank you" and crawled back into bed. My hands were shaking uncontrollably from the scare.

"This has been happening more and more," said Nick. "You should have your thyroid checked again. Let me go and grab you a glass of water."

Deep down I was aware that cutting pills in half and waking up with this type of choking attack had nothing to do with thyroid issues.

Once Nick was back under the covers next to me, I moved into his embrace. It didn't take him long to fall asleep, and I focused on listening to his comforting, light snoring to help soothe me back into as normal a sleep as I could enjoy.

Graytown originally was named for a man called Captain John Grey, and the spelling was originally Greytown. In recent years, it was changed to Graytown, as if the town itself wanted to break free from its original ancestry.

Captain Grey helped the town erect a magnificent lighthouse in the bay, a New England monolith that had safely guided ships through these treacherous waters for years, and had once been the town's pride and joy. It still greeted all who entered via the one road that led into and out of our quaint little town.

Coincidently, the Grey Lighthouse had been a working lighthouse until just a month after your death, Hope, when the town and the private investors no longer had the resources to keep it running. When I came back to Graytown so many years later, the Grey Lighthouse was the first familiar "face" to greet me, although by then it reflected the many years of neglect with a gray, dismal feel. The Fresnel lens high up in the tower still appeared to be the ever-watchful eye, watching over the bay and this town.

Maybe someday that lighthouse will be restored to her original state, with her lens cleaned and once again shining brightly through clouds, the overcast skies, and the thickest fog, and guiding boats through the bay. Without it, only the power of God can determine when the bay, the town, and my home would be bathed in sunshine, and when it would be shrouded in impenetrable gloom.

As I moved to the sink to empty the day-old coffee down the drain, I caught a glimpse of the sun trying to break through the clouds. A streak of light fell on a small pile of brightly colored leaves gathered around the trunk of the oak tree, bathing them in an amber glow and casting forth vivid colors of red, yellow, orange, green, and specks of brown.

Soon enough, all these leaves would wither away and lose their beauty and it would be time to rake them up and dispose of them in the woods. There, in their little brown piles, they would slowly rot away and cycle back into the ground. My heart skipped a beat, as this vision and time of year forced my thoughts to wander to one of the last moments of your life.

And then I could see you, standing there by the oak tree outside my window, picking up one of the newly dropped orange-red leaves and twirling it by its stem, around and around. I could feel my heart beating faster, and I forced my eyes back to the sink below, at the running water overflowing the coffee pot in my hand. I tried desperately to ignore the vision and calm my mind, but no matter how hard I tried, I just couldn't escape the haunting memories. My thoughts drifted on, to the last afternoon I spent with your mother.

"Can you please refill my glass with more water, dear?" asked Mrs. Marksman, even though she was sitting at the kitchen table not far from the sink.

I was raised to obey my elders, so I took the glass from her hand and walked over to the sink. I no longer needed to stand on the tiny metal step stool with the black rubber tread on top, located only a few steps away. As the water rushed out of the faucet and into the glass, my twelve-year-old eyes, no longer innocent, looked out the kitchen window at the large oak tree. Your mother had already taken a few of the large pills inside the bottle, and had a few more in her hand. With my hand shaking ever so slightly, I handed her the glass of water.

"Thank you, sweetie. Would you be so kind as to check back to see me before dinner tonight?" Mrs. Marksman asked.

"Yes, Mrs. Marksman," I stammered.

Before washing down the pills with water, she put the glass and pills down and rested her hands on top of a closed green spiral notebook. A black pen lay close by. I noticed that she always kept her fingernails cut short and square so they all matched perfectly, and that she wore only clear polish. I could smell the aloe hand cream she used constantly throughout the day. She sat there in her long, blue fleece nightgown, with a striped blue and white bathrobe tied loosely over it. Her cozy slippers were pale pink.

She had always been an average-sized woman, but she had lost at least thirty pounds since her daughter's death. Since your death. Now, all her clothes fit loosely for those few occasions she dressed to leave the house. Her long, straight, auburn hair had always been pulled back into a bun until the week prior to this particular day, when she cut and donated her hair. My mother had offered to take her shopping for a new outfit to celebrate her new haircut, but Mrs. Marksman's glassy blue eyes stared back, as she uttered, "Perhaps another day." Most of the town viewed this hair-cutting milestone as a sign that she was finally coming out of her state of mourning, almost a year after her daughter's death.

"I want to tell you something, Jean. Can you promise me you'll never forget what I'm about to tell you?" Mrs. Marksman asked.

"Yes, ma'am," I replied.

She hesitated, then picked a well-worn soft-cover play of *Hamlet* that had been lying on the table next to her. She leafed absently through the pages a few times. It was the same play she had used for years in her high school English curriculum. After she collected her thoughts, she closed the book, rested her hands on top of it, and addressed me.

"Whatever you do in life, please promise me you'll not be another tragically flawed Hamlet. Hamlet never did the things he should have done, because he believed he was a victim of fate. But he always had the choice to act, to make decisions, and that was the real tragedy. I don't believe in fate, Jean. I believe in free will."

I was wondering how I should respond, when she opened the copy of Hamlet again, took out a few photographs that had been tucked between pages, and placed these on the table in front of me. The pictures were of you and me when we were around nine years old. We were both standing on the old child-sized red worn picnic table in my yard, dressed in my mother's old dresses, hats, and jewelry, and covered in horribly applied makeup. We had sand-filled blue shakers in our hands, and we were acting out a musical routine we'd worked on for hours. Even though our mothers weren't in the pictures, both of them had been sitting on lawn chairs in our "front-row seating" section, and one of them had taken those pictures as we happily performed for them.

"I always told you girls the entire world is your stage," said Mrs. Marksman. "Only you can decide which play to act out."

I hadn't realized at the time, but she was talking about Shakespeare's play *As You Like It*. I smiled up at her and listened intently.

"Free will led to Hope's death, and to the death of your childhood innocence." She fixed me with her somber eyes, then continued, "In another play, *Macbeth*, Shakespeare talks about spots, the victim's blood, that could not be washed out. I walked for years with stains like that, and I don't want you to do the same. So Jean, I'm telling you to accept today as a blank sheet, and to live a long, happy life."

Then she opened the green spiral notebook, tore out a blank piece of blue-lined white paper, slid it carefully across the table to rest just above the pictures placed in front of me, and smiled.

I had not seen your mother smile in almost a year – since before your death and giving up her English teaching position at the local high school, so she could shut herself in this house and away from the plays and literature she loved.

In my heart, your mother's words and smile granted me the forgiveness I had been longing for.

I smiled back and graciously accepted the symbolic sheet of paper. I folded the page twice and placed it in my left jacket pocket. After a few more polite words, I left your mother sitting in the kitchen chair and headed home to work on my homework and prepare for dinner.

A few hours later, I looked up from my social studies book, distracted by the smell of tuna casserole, my favorite meal, baking in the kitchen. It was my chore to set the table for dinner, and so I headed downstairs.

As I entered the kitchen, I found my mother quietly humming while she cooked dinner. I found her song comforting and didn't want to interrupt her, so I reached into the cabinets and started my nightly chore. Then I glanced at the kitchen clock above the jelly cabinet and noticed it was close to five o'clock. Remembering my promise to go next door around dinnertime to check on Mrs. Marksman, I hurried to finish setting the table. Then I went to grab my blue jacket off the wire hanger in the hall closet. As I ran out the door, I yelled to my mother that I'd be back in a few minutes.

The storm door slammed behind me as I skipped down the newly built wooden front porch, with its six extra-long steps. There were two ways to reach your side porch. The first was the proper, courteous way that I never chose to take. This way involved walking down our paved walkway and driveway, through the circle and into your driveway, up the stairs from the sunken driveway with high walls, and then across the short walkway to the base of the side porch.

Or, there was the much shorter and direct route that I preferred, cutting through my mother's garden, across our lawn, and around the small fence of growing green bushes that covered about half of the cleared area between our houses.

After I was around the small path of dividing trees, I climbed the side steps. I was relieved to see that your father's red Ford truck wasn't in the driveway. I carefully climbed the steep side porch stairs. After ringing the doorbell a few times, I stood there waiting and hoping your mother would appear. When she didn't, my heart sank in my chest. I was chilled as the cool air swept by, and I heard myself breathing heavily as I reached up to open the storm door. After knocking on the big wooden brown door behind the storm door, for what seemed like an eternity, I turned the doorknob to see if it was locked. The door was unlocked, so I invited myself into the den.

Out of the corner of my eye, I caught a glimpse of your navy blue backpack tucked carefully beneath the little table next to the living room couch. I'd never noticed that it had sat there all this time, untouched since your death over a year ago. The lucky white rabbit's foot I'd given to you was still hanging from the metal zipper.

I was filled with fear and needed your strength to help guide me along, so I impulsively unclipped the rabbit's foot and held it firmly in my fist. My palm started to sweat, soaking the soft white fur as I clutched it hard, trying to draw out enough strength to move past the den. Part of me wanted to run home and ask one of my parents to come over and check on your mother, but I wanted to prove to you that I wasn't weak.

With my heart racing, I crept through the kitchen and croaked a timid "Hello?" As I passed the table, I noticed that the notebook and pen were missing, along with all the pill bottles from earlier. I slowly moved down the small hallway off the kitchen, turned, and climbed the grey carpeted staircase which led to three upstairs bedrooms and two bathrooms.

Since your death, your mother rarely slept in her bedroom. I knew this because the bed in your room was constantly left unmade. One day I had gone into your room to search for your old blue felted Campfire Girl's vest, decorated with noble patches and beads, and noticed that the pillow on your bed was covered in the pillowcase matching your parents' bedroom comforter set we'd both admired.

Even though I was a child, I'd heard the quiet gossip of the townspeople, whispers that after you died your father rarely came home most nights. And when he did, the slipshod way he parked the car suggested that it was a small miracle he'd made it home at all.

Your mother believed that her one obligation was to mourn you, and it was apparent she had no desire to salvage a marriage that was beyond repair. As the town gossip spread, I learned that your father's first indiscretions had started long before, but that your death was what triggered his alcoholism.

Passing your parents' room, I noticed that the door was slightly ajar. My heart raced as I pushed it open and saw your mother in her bed. I moved across the room, trying to wake her by calling out, "Mrs. Marksman? Mrs. Marksman?" Out of the corner of my eye, I could see the empty orange pill bottle with the white label on it, tipped over on the nightstand next to an empty large drinking glass. The white childproof cap was on the floor beside the bed.

I stood and stared at her face. Her eyes were closed and her skin was gray. With my trembling hand, I reached down and tried to feel for a pulse. Her skin was cold, and I knew she was beyond help. I could smell the foul stench from her last bodily excretions.

A lot of people go through life and never have to find a dead body. By age twelve, I had witnessed the death of my best friend and discovered the lifeless body of her mother.

She held, clutched tightly in her cold hands, a sealed envelope with the words, "To Whom It May Concern" written neatly across the back. I knew I would need both hands, so I unzipped my left jacket pocket and shoved the white rabbit's foot into it. As I reached inside, I felt the folded piece of paper Mrs. Marksman had given me.

Free will and a clean slate.

With unsteady hands and tears streaming down my face, I managed to free the envelope, stared at it for a moment, then folded it and slipped it into the pocket with my other treasures of the day and zipped it shut.

I ran back to your room, but caught myself just outside the door. The bed was nicely made, and the room was dusted and vacuumed. A box with my name written on it sat at the foot of the bed, along with a few other boxes marked with the names of family members.

I choked back a sob as it dawned on me that she had been sleeping in your bed for all these months, but tonight she chose to end her life in her own.

I carefully opened each of the labeled boxes to make sure there were no other letters. To my relief, they held only small sentimental trinkets that had belonged to you. Then I took the boxes and piled them neatly in the bedroom closet – including the one addressed to me.

Without a note, without proof of planning, people could only speculate.

On the way back to your parents' bedroom, it all began to catch up with me. Trying hard to control my crying, I picked up the yellow phone on the nightstand next to the bed and dialed 911 on the rotary dial.

As it rang, I let my body fall against the wall next to the nightstand and slid down onto the floor, cradling my legs against my chest.

"Nine-one-one, state your emergency."

I unzipped the pocket, found the rabbit's foot and gripped it tightly.

"She's dead," I sobbed.

"All right now, I'm here to help you. What's the address, please?"

"813 Graze Street, I think. It's the house before mine which is 815."

"What's your name?"

"It's Jean."

"Jean, I'm Joyce, how old are you, honey?"

"Twelve."

"Jean, are you alone? Are there any adults with you?"

"I'm alone. I checked in and found her..."

"Help's on the way, Jean. Are there any injuries visible? Any blood?"

"No. No, it's like she's sleeping."

"Did you check for a pulse? Can I walk you through CPR?"

"She's gray and her lips are blue. She messed herself in the bed. I can smell it."

"Do you know her name, Jean?"

"It's Mrs. Marksman."

"How old do you think Mrs. Marksman is?"

"My mom's age, I guess. Around thirty-five."

"All right Jean, you can put the phone down, but please don't hang up. Can you go and open the door for the medical team?"

"The side door is unlocked."

"Okay, Jean, I'm telling them to come in the side door. Where are you and Mrs. Marksman in the house?"

"We're upstairs in her bedroom. First room on the right."

I could hear the sirens coming closer. They were the same siren sounds as when the ambulance was finally called for you. Then it was all too much for me, and I vomited all over the rose-colored bedroom rug.

The sound of the doorbell jarred me back to the present.

Wiping away tears with the back of my hands, I headed down the hallway toward the front door. The doorbell rang again. "Coming!" I shouted.

As I took the doorknob in my hand, I thought I could hear a faint giggling, the music of two happy young girls, rising, swirling, then fading away on the gusts of wind outside.

I opened the heavy oak door, my mouth set in that empty smile specially designed to greet visitors, only to be met with nothing but my own reflection in the glass of the storm door. I stepped out onto the porch and peered down the street in both directions, but there was no one in sight.

Behind a bush by the road I thought I caught a glimpse of two eight-year-olds, you and me, crouched down and smothering laughter with our hands. I sighed, fondly remembering the fun we had ringing doorbells and hiding nearby. As I watched, a pair of sparrows spiraled up out of the bush and flew away. I sighed again and went back into the house, pulling the door shut behind me.

When I got back in the kitchen I sat on the floor, Indian-style, resting my back against the wall near the breakfast table. I stared for what seemed like hours through the window over the kitchen sink, through the top of the oak tree, and watched the white clouds swirling behind it.

My reverie ended when Meg burst in through the door from the garage, wearing a lovely black hat and carrying her black backpack slung over her shoulder. "What are you doing?"

"I'm playing around with yoga poses," I replied.

"Really mom?" she said. "You hate yoga."

I laughed. "Hey, baby girl," I said, "That's what you think. I've been practicing 'down dog.' Want to join me?

Meg shook her head. "Mother. You are so not funny when you say stuff like that."

"Yes I am," I said, smiling sweetly. "Love the hat, honey. Where'd you get it?"

She mumbled something I couldn't quite make out, threw the hat and backpack on a kitchen chair, and dashed up the stairs toward her bedroom.

It occurred to me that some people, like Meg, could pull off wearing hats and always manage to look good in them, while others simply could not – like Mrs. Bellows, the eccentric local woman known for her assortment of strange headwear. Mrs. Bellows had married briefly at age eighteen, and even though the marriage was almost immediately annulled, she chose for the rest of her life to stay a "Mrs." and to wear her fleeting husband's name like just one more hat.

As I got to my feet, struggling a bit, I heard the garage door open. I was still standing by the sink, deciding between a pot of fresh coffee and a bottle of water, when Nick came through the door. He had his suit jacket slung over his shoulder by one finger, his briefcase in the other hand, and he carried the mail awkwardly in his mouth. "Mfff mffff mfff," he said.

I laughed. "What?"

He tossed his jacket on top of Meg's backpack, then took the mail out of his mouth and tossed it on the table. "I said, hey there beautiful, were you just standing there waiting for me?"

I laughed again. "I bet you say that to all the women."

"Only the beautiful ones. Who are standing around waiting for me."

We both laughed, and I stood on my tippy toes to wrap my arms around my husband's neck. Even so, my face barely reached his collarbone. He pulled me in close for a kiss, then pushed back a bit to look at me with those piercing blue eyes. He brushed a few brown strands of hair off my face and leaned down to kiss me again.

I think both of us were considering the possibility of taking things well beyond a simple kiss, but Meg brought us back down to earth. "Seriously? Get a room, you two. There's a sleazy motel just up the road. Oh, but before you do, Dad, can you drop me off at Lisa's house on your way to play hoops with the guys?" For some reason she rolled her eyes and put air quotes around the word "guys."

I was just working up steam for a good solid mom-rant about teenage girls respecting their parents, when Nick rescued our daughter by planting a kiss on my forehead. "Jean, there's absolutely no denying that this girl is your daughter," he said. "Only when you get snotty, it's somehow a lot more attractive."

My anger slipped away, and I shook my head at Meg. "You do realize that if your father wasn't around I'd probably be sending you off to military school for girls, right? You've lost a lot of your childlike charm since you hit puberty."

"Yeah, well I'm sure that after living here, I could handle it. Oh, and I'll bet there's a boys' military school just around the corner. Hmm, doesn't sound so bad," said Meg.

Nick chuckled. "Nope, no military school for you - or guys. Just give me a few minutes to change, and I'll drop you off at Lisa's."

"Thanks, Dad," Meg said over her shoulder as she scampered back up the stairs with her long, perfectly styled light brown hair swaying from side to side.

She had inherited Nick's height, and already towered over me at nearly five-nine. She was extremely thin, and had long legs that she liked to accentuate with heels. Still, she generally dressed appropriately for her age. She had my high cheek bones and dark brown eyes, with Nick's long eyelashes. She was born with her father's perfect smile, and had never needed braces or a retainer.

After Meg and Nick left, I began sorting through the mail while I planned dinner in my head. I had tossed the last grocery store circular back on the table and picked up Nick's jacket to hang it up, when Meg's backpack caught my eye.

The top of the backpack was partially unzipped, revealing a folded envelope that was on the verge of falling out. My heart raced, and I could feel myself being drawn back again to that sealed letter addressed, "To Whom it May Concern."

The letter had stayed in my blue jacket pocket for three days, as I tried to decide what to do with it. I had periodically unzipped the pocket to make sure it was still there, but I never took it out to read it. Mrs. Marksman must have counted on me finding her that night, along with the note. Somehow she needed to confess in writing, maybe to ease her own pain. If she had intended it for her husband, she would have written, "For Damian" on the envelope.

I had been afraid to open the letter, to read it, or to hand it over to the authorities. I didn't even want to go to my parents with it. I felt that it was important to protect your mother – and you – from the gossip and scorn your mother's last message could ignite. There was already enough talk going around about your father and his indiscretions, about his drinking. And too many whispers about you.

I was the only one who knew it existed, and I intended to keep it that way.

Three nights later, I waited for my parents to fall asleep, then quietly got dressed in a dark red t-shirt and jeans, with thick white socks and white Keds sneakers. Of course, I wore that same blue jacket. The only other supplies I took with me were a single package of matches and a flashlight.

I could hear my parents and our golden retriever snoring in their bedroom as I tiptoed down the wooden staircase.

It took what seemed like an hour to slowly, silently twist the brass door lock, holding my body close to it to mask any telltale sound. I quietly opened the storm door and gently eased it closed behind me. Out on the porch, I froze as the automatic sensor lights came on, waiting for the house to light up and to hear my father shout, "Who's there?"

But the house stayed dark, and there was no shout, only a particularly loud snore from my parents' window, so I tiptoed down the porch steps and across the yard.

The woods, not really all that inviting during the day, were terrifying at night. Pitch black shadows formed pits of pure evil that seemed to retreat from the weak light of my flashlight. The only thing more ominous than the woods that night was the name of my destination, a place that the older kids called Dead Man's Peak.

For years, the older kids had tried to scare the younger ones with stories about Dead Man's Peak and the Bog Man who lived there. According to the legend, he was an old man with a wild beard and piercing, beady, blue eyes. He had a BB gun, and he would shoot and try to kidnap any child who ventured too close to an invisible "boundary line" part way up the hill that protected his lair. According to the stories, the Bog Man had captured a child named Luke twenty years back, and nobody was sure if Luke was dead or alive.

We could see the hill to Dead Man's Peak, and the top of the peak itself from our "Mystery Solvers Club" headquarters, a tree fort we'd built. The Mystery Solvers had often found old BB pellets near the boundary line, and a few of the older boys showed us marks and scars on themselves to prove that they'd been shot by the Bog Man and barely escaped capture. They convinced us they'd never try again to go past the forbidden boundary.

It was, of course, all done to discourage us from learning the truth.

Just a few months before your death, four of us fell into the trap of a "triple dog dare" to learn once and for all if the legend was true. Danny, Timmy, Michael, and I were supposed to race through the woods to see if we could get the Bog Man to chase us. Katie stayed behind, in case she had to go for help.

We ran with our hearts pounding, past the boundary and up the hill, halfway ready to feel the sting of a BB or to run even faster from a bearded apparition. Then we reached the top of the hill, and discovered the truth behind the legend.

Just over the peak of the hill was a good-sized depression, forming a sort of pit with sturdy mud walls. The pit was littered with empty beer cans, pornographic magazines, and trash from food wrappers. In the center, there was a large stone fire ring.

So we all survived our dare unscathed, except for little Timmy, who suffered a humiliation that would follow him around for months. Michael, who showed no fear at all, had raced well ahead of us. Near the top, he abruptly turned and ran back down, screaming "I'm shot! The Bog Man shot me!" When he threw himself down onto a bed of leaves, pine needles, and dirt at Timmy's feet, groaning in agony, poor Timmy wet his pants.

I found myself wishing that I'd brought along your lucky rabbit's foot, but I'd taken it out of the jacket pocket, along with the symbolic blank page. I heard an owl hoot, and the leaves on the trees rustled in the faint breeze. The air was cool, and I could see my breath in the damp night air. Finally, I reached the top of Dead Man's Peak, and went to work.

I scanned the flashlight around to find a handful of dried leaves, twigs, and pine needles, and arranged these in the center of the fire pit. I pulled out the matchbook, lifted up its cardboard cover, and tore off a match. The first match didn't light, crumbling in my shaky hand. The second match flared up, and I dropped it carefully onto my pile of kindling. Then I retrieved the letter from my other pocket, unfolded it, and I prepared to drop in onto the fire.

Just as I released it, I was startled by movement near me. A person holding a flashlight was standing in a long, dark shadow not far from the fire pit, and my first thought was that it had to be a ghost or a witch. It was, after all, the "witching hour."

Then I heard a familiar voice. "What on earth are you doing out here? You'd better not be trying some kind of pagan ritual to try to bring back your dead friend." Mrs. Bellows, wearing a peculiar red hat and a very large frown, stepped out of the shadow and into the faint light from my little fire.

"No, no, ma'am," I stammered.

"Well, what are you doing with this fire then?"

I looked into the pit and noticed that her distraction had caused the letter to fall just outside the flames, so that the corner of it was just barely singed. Mrs. Bellows reached into her big purse and pulled out a glass jar filled with colorful layers of sand, opened it, and dumped its contents over the fire. "My daughter made this sand art for me," she said. "Still, it's better than letting you burn down the forest."

I didn't know what to do. I figured that she'd drag me back to my parents, or even the authorities. Instead, she cocked her head to one side and asked, "What's in this letter you came all this way to burn?"

"I'm not sure, ma'am."

She played the light from her flashlight on the letter, and leaned down to take a closer look. I could see her eyebrows raise as she read the words, "To Whom It May Concern," in Mrs. Marksman's neat, round handwriting. But Mrs. Bellows' response was not what I expected; she simply straightened up, forced a weak smile, and said, "We'll never speak of this again. Let sleeping dogs lie."

"Yes, ma'am. Thank you, Mrs. Bellows," I said.

As she walked me back to the edge of the woods, I could see the yellow-green back porch light turned on at Mr. Raven's house, lighting up the stretch of woods that divided the Marksman's house from ours. Mr. Raven was widowed without children, and was rumored to finally be dating someone again. All the evidence pointed to Mrs. Bellows being the mystery woman. She must have been leaving Mr. Raven's home, spotted me moving through the woods, and decided to follow me to the pit.

Mrs. Bellows was an attractive woman, but instead of being admired for her beauty, she made herself stand out by wearing odd hats and eclectic clothes. She was thin, with brown shoulder-length hair and beautiful hazel eyes. She had a round face with almost flawless porcelain skin. Her ears were perfect-sized, and when her hair was pushed behind them, these were probably her best feature. I remember overhearing my mother comment at a Christmas party one year that it was a shame Mrs. Bellows never wore earrings.

She didn't drive, but always walked or took a taxi around town.

She was a born-again Christian who loved to recite Bible verses condemning any perceived sin by the children in the neighborhood, especially if that sin included mocking or teasing her daughter, Isabella. Isabella suffered mental handicaps and had to live in an assisted living facility miles outside of town. Mrs. Bellows had raised Isabella, keeping the identity of her daughter's father a secret. My group of friends never teased Isabella, but we'd witnessed the older crowd of teenagers mocking her in the past and had witnessed the biblical wrath of Mrs. Bellows.

Her house was at the end of our road, on the opposite corner from my house, where most of the traffic flowed into our neighborhood. On this night, the place was dark and uninviting, with nothing to light her way home, so after she left me on my porch, she set off back into the night guided only by her flashlight.

Back in bed and safely under the covers, I lay awake, worrying about what would become of the letter. I expected the authorities to show up at our house, and maybe even arrest me for tampering with a crime scene and removing evidence.

Finally, somehow, I did manage to fall asleep that night.

When I climbed back up to Dead Man's Peak the next day, there was no evidence of my fire in the pit, and the letter was gone. Mrs. Bellows must have gone back to retrieve it. I stood and looked into the pit, confused by a combination of fear and gratitude toward Mrs. Bellows. She had swept up the colored sand from her daughter's artwork, along with all the ashes from my fire and from the fires of many years gone by. Why? Had she finished my job and burned the letter, or taken it away with the sand and ashes?

I sat on a log bordering the pit, surrounded by pine trees barely moving in the breeze. An earthy-brown sparrow landed on one of the pine branches, singing a song that perfectly mirrored my sorrow.

Every year, on the last Saturday in June, Graytown holds the annual Town Bonfire. When I was thirteen years old, the Bonfire fell on June 25, the day my family had scheduled our move to our new home in Derry, New Hampshire, to accommodate my father's new job in Manchester. My parents decided to delay the move by one day and leave on Sunday so that we could go to the Bonfire, and I could see my friends one more time.

June 25 was also Gloria Marksman's birthday, a fact burned into my memory by the "in loving memory" bookmark I had brought home from her burial service.

Most thirteen-year-olds would plead not to move away from a town that was the only home they had ever known, but I was ready to close that chapter of my life, leave childhood behind, and move on. Years later, I would learn that my father had taken the job in Manchester specifically to get me away from Graytown and the constant reminders of my pain.

But the last thing I wanted to see on my last day in town was a raging bonfire.

Just about everybody in town was there. The manicured lawn was littered with families sitting on sheets, blankets, and an assortment of chairs. Kids ran around waving sparklers, parents drank coffee, and children drank hot cocoa out of thermoses. A local band played music, while a few couples and children laughed and danced without a care in the world.

As I sat there in the grass, listening to the band, and watched all the happy people around me, I could feel my unhappiness growing heavier and heavier with each passing minute, pressing down on my shoulders and chest, silently crushing me under the sky of that warm summer evening. Each orange and red flame dancing in the fire haunted me.

It would be nearly ten years after that night before I would be able to enjoy a bonfire.

My parents hired professional movers to transport most of our belongings to our new home in Derry. In addition to the movers and the moving trucks, my father's brother, Dougie, offered to drive a small van for us.

As my parents and I backed out of our Graze Street driveway for the last time in our blue Pontiac Grand Prix, I sat in the back seat patting our golden retriever, Rosie, on the head. My other arm rested on top of the cat carrier that held our black cat, Peppermint Patty. As we passed by your house, I caught a glimpse of your father sitting on the front porch stairs, drinking a beer and surrounded by empty cans.

Damian Marksman was a tall, ruggedly handsome man, with the beginnings of a receding hairline. His red pickup truck, with a recently smashed-in passenger-side taillight, was parked nearly crossways in the driveway.

Even from the distance I could see a glint of sunlight reflected in his dark blue eyes, eyes that always held that deep color, even when he was wearing greens or grays. They were your eyes too, Hope.

My father beeped the horn, and we all waved good-bye to your father. I thought to myself that this would be the last time I'd ever see him. I didn't know back then that a statement to live by is, "Never say never."

Autumn

Red flames danced
As the white envelope
With black penned ink fell
Trying to silence the voice whose story it was to tell
A lamb's choice breathes air to the fire below
Shifting from shielded innocence
To the heavy stature of a lioness
Defining a choice and one's free will
The catcher of lost souls
A saddened sparrow weeps
As colored beach sand tears freely flow

Chapter II

In the months since your ghost first appeared to me, I discovered that sitting at the table every morning, drinking black coffee and gazing at the apparition of a young child seemed normal. I decided to give up any sense of fear and embrace your presence, to welcome my time alone with a very old friend.

In fact, over time our visits had become oddly therapeutic. I discovered I could, after all these years, say your name out loud. I will admit, though, that the first time you showed up was traumatic.

I was heading back to the table with a mug of coffee in my hand and my current novel on my mind, and there you sat on that brown kitchen chair, wearing your white confirmation dress and staring silently at me. I stood there, frozen, trapped somewhere between curiosity and terror, then the coffee mug slipped from my hand. I glanced down at the shattered remains of my mug, and when I looked back up you were gone.

I cleaned up the mess and decided not to tell anyone about your visit.

At first, I thought your ghost might be dropping in to complain about the fact that I had taken down your confirmation photograph, the one that stood on the mantle in the den for years, and stashed it in a desk drawer. I told myself that it was a simple decision about room decor, but I think I was also trying not to be reminded of you every day.

As your visits became more frequent, my fear evaporated, replaced with a kind of gratitude that you were giving me some time with you. I decided that you were coming around to help me sort out my feelings, to let me deal with the sadness that was crushing me. After all, you did send all those messages to your mother and me right after your funeral. You made sure we knew that you were in a better place, and watching over us.

It was autumn, and the butterflies should have all been long gone by the time we took your body up to Ansel Cemetery. Yet as I stood there, watching them lower your small coffin into your grave, a perfect monarch landed on my shoulder, a magnificent study in red, orange, and yellow, all framed in an outline of black.

Your mother saw it, and she stopped crying. Her face relaxed into a look of peace at the beauty of the butterfly. A golden light burst through the two oak trees flanking the entrance to the cemetery, warming us all with a sense of courage. These oak trees were so different from the one in your yard.

The next night, your parents had my family over for dinner at your house. As we all sat around the brown kitchen table, my mother said grace: "Thank you, God, for the food we're about to eat. Please take care of Hope, our darling child you have called back into your presence. Amen."

My father said, "Amen," and reached for the salad bowl.

"Wait," I said, "can I add something?"

"Of course," my mother replied. My father set the salad down and we all bowed our heads.

"Dear God," I said, "it's me, Jean Cartwright. Can you please have Hope watch over me, and over the rest of us here tonight? Amen."

Everyone responded with another "Amen," then your mother stood up and wiped a tear from her eye.

"Excuse me, please," she said. "I forgot to put out the pepper shaker."

When she opened the door to the spice cabinet, a blue butterfly outlined in black flew out past her head and fluttered toward the hallway. Your mother let out a little yelp of surprise, and I forgot my manners, jumping up from my seat shouting, "Wow, did you see that?"

My mother went over and put a comforting arm around your mother, and we all stood transfixed for a few seconds, watching the butterfly head down the hallway and toward the staircase. Then I ran to the hall door and said, "Well shouldn't we follow it? It has to be a sign!"

"Yes, maybe we should," said your mother. Before any of us could make it to the kitchen door, though, the butterfly reached the bottom of the stairs, hovered for an instant, and vanished.

For the next few weeks, we seemed to see butterflies everywhere we went, until the first chill of the winter to come chased even them away.

I sipped my coffee and smiled at your ghost. "Nick and I met in college. Remember how we used to laugh about how we were going to meet our husbands? It was just like one of our stories. I had your lucky white rabbit's foot attached to my backpack, you know, when I slipped on a patch of ice in front of the library and fell on my... my rear end."

I took another sip and looked into your expressionless eyes, then I went on. "Back then, of course, we all had to go to the library to use the computers to type our papers. So there I sat on the sidewalk, with my books and papers scattered around me, and Nick showed up, a gallant knight riding up to save a fair maiden in distress. When he helped me to my feet, I looked into his blue eyes, saw that dimple when he smiled, and it was love at first sight. I can tell you, Hope, it does exist!"

Then it dawned on me that you never lived long enough to go on your first date, much less get married. So I sat there silently sipping my coffee and looking back at you, wondering if I should tell you how wonderful my life became the moment I left this town and became a normal teenager.

Once we got settled in Derry, my parents credited the improvement in my mood to counseling. It did help, of course, but there were some things that I didn't care to tell any of my therapists, so I personally decided that my success had more to do with pushing all these things so far down in my mind, burying them so deeply, that they could never come back to hurt me again.

As I grew through my teen years, I often thought about your parents. I knew that they had been high school sweethearts who got married. When we were younger, it was one of the themes in the little love stories we made up for our future selves. I think we were both aware, though, of the tension between your mother and father.

Thinking back on my last conversation with your mother, I couldn't help thinking that one of the indelible stains in her life might have been her marriage.

When Meg was about three years old, I received a certified letter from Damian Marksman, followed by a phone call from his lawyer, Walter Smith. The letter explained that your father was in a hospital in Florida, not expected to live much longer, and that I had been named executrix of his estate. In addition, I was to inherit the house in Graytown, all of its contents, and the college fund your parents had maintained for you. I was to fly to Florida to meet with Mr. Smith to discuss the details.

At the time, Nick and I were living in a small two-bedroom apartment within walking distance of downtown Concord, NH.

We had only one car, and had not saved nearly enough money for a house.

My conversation with the lawyer had been brief. I stood in the kitchen of our apartment, listening carefully and twisting the cord of the green wall phone. Mr. Smith told me that the only stipulation for inheriting everything would be to see you father face-to-face, one last time.

Of course, Nick was suspicious. "Why would this stranger leave everything to you? There must be some serious strings attached."

"He's not a stranger. His daughter, Hope, was my best friend. I saw her die in a horrible accident when we were eleven. I was also the one who found her mother a year later...after...well... she took too many pills. Mr. Marksman kind of crawled into a bottle of liquor after all that."

"Have you been in contact with him all this time?"

"No, I haven't seen him since the day we moved away from Graytown."

"Why didn't you tell me about all this?"

"It's not something I want to relive. Not even with you. Sorry."

Nick took my hand. "No, I'm sorry. Still, I should be there with you. I'm just not sure I can get off work. I don't trust this guy."

"Did you know that you can't steer a sailboat if the centerboard is broken?" I asked.

Nick laughed. "What does that have to do with anything?"

"Actually, everything. When I was little, my father took me out on a sailboat – a small one, called a Skate. We were a long way from shore, and the centerboard broke off. My father had been sailing since he was a boy, and he still couldn't find any way to steer that boat. Lucky for us, some teenagers came along and towed us in."

Nick shook his head. "I don't get it."

I took his hand. "The point is, I think it just kind of broke Mr. Marksman's centerboard when Hope and her mother died, and he lost control of his life. Maybe now that he's at the end, he's just trying to get it back on course."

Nick smiled and shook his head again. "Maybe you should write a book. You never cease to amaze me with your stories."

"I think I might just do that," I replied.

Looking across the kitchen table into your ghostly face, your father's eyes staring back at me send a chill down my spine. "Hope, can you tell me why you waited so long to visit me?"

Oddly, the thing I remember most about your father's hospital room is the little white vase of fake daisies on the windowsill. I looked at them and wondered if they had come from a friend, if he even had any friends, or if one of the duty nurses had put them there as an act of kindness to a dying patient.

All the way to Florida, I had struggled with the idea of facing your father. While I blamed myself for the part I played in your death, I blamed your father for what happened to your mother. If he had been a better husband, a better man, your mother might not have committed suicide.

And I was not entirely convinced that my sailboat analogy was correct. I still had a nagging suspicion that there was something in this I was not seeing. My one consolation was that I would not be completely isolated; the lawyer, Mr. Smith, would be just outside the room.

On the way from the airport to the hospital, Mr. Smith told me that Damian had been living in a condominium in Florida for the past ten years, but that he'd kept the house in Graytown. He'd had it cleaned weekly by a professional cleaning company, and hired landscapers to keep the yard in the summer and clear the snow in the winter. He had kept the heat and power on, and all the bills and taxes paid.

Yet he had never set foot in that house since the day he left for Florida.

"Mr. Smith," I asked, "did Mr. Marksman say why he wouldn't sell the house in Graytown? It seems strange that he wouldn't even rent it out."

"Mrs. Rhodes, as a lawyer I have learned not to ask questions to which I do not require an answer," said Mr. Smith.

So there in your father's room, lying in a bed not far from that vase of fake daisies, was a thin old man. He was almost completely bald, and liver spots nearly covered his head and face, a testament to many years of exposure to the Florida sun. He had an IV tube taped to his left arm, and a morphine infusion button near his right hand. A cardiac monitor behind the IV stand beeped rhythmically.

At first, I thought I had wandered into the wrong room. But there, buried in that wizened face were those deep, dark blue eyes.

"Jean Cartwright, is that you?"

"Yes, Mr. Marksman, it's me."

"Thanks for making the trip." He coughed a little, grimacing in pain.

"You really didn't give me much choice," I said.

He gathered his strength and smiled weakly. "You must be curious why I'm leaving it all to you."

"To be truthful, that thought did cross my mind. I'm still waiting for the other shoe to drop."

He shook his head. "Jean, there's no other shoe. You were Hope's best friend, and I want you to have that damned house and everything in it."

"But why?"

"I won't be taking anything with me where I'm going."

"Isn't there anything inside the house you want me to give to relatives or friends?" I asked.

"What relatives? What friends? I closed out Hope's college fund, too. It was Gloria's idea to start it..." He paused and squeezed his eyes shut.

"Um, sure," I said. "My parents had one for me too."

He opened his eyes, but this time they were focused on nothing. "You just had to insist on stretching things, didn't you?" he shouted. "It was the night after that argument that he happened. You forced me to leave for the night, remember? Future planning all right, goddammit! Well, that worked out perfectly now, didn't it?"

The beeping of the monitor sped up, and the nurse came into the room. She spoke calmly and softly to your father as she checked the IV bottle and fluffed his pillow. "All right now, Mr. Marksman. It's Nurse Linzi. We need to calm down now, Mr. Marksman. You have a visitor." She glanced at her watch, then reached over and pressed the morphine button.

He closed his eyes again and his breathing began to slow. The nurse took my elbow and guided me over near the door. "Please try to keep him as calm as possible. He tends to get sort of agitated, and he's pretty fragile," she whispered.

"Of course. Thank you," I said.

On her way out the door she called back over her shoulder "Mr. Marksman, enjoy your visit. I'll be just outside if you need me again."

Your father grunted, then opened his eyes. It took him a few seconds to focus on me. "Sorry. My mind wanders sometimes. What were we talking about?"

I forced a smile. "I was just thanking you for your generosity, Mr. Marksman."

He smiled back. "You're welcome." He gazed at me for a few seconds, then said, "Jean, you and I have spent all these years blaming each other for the things that happened. Now I need to stop blaming and find some peace if I'm ever going to have a chance to spend eternity with my family." He coughed, flinched, and gave the morphine button another press.

I bit my lip. "Well, I pray that you will see Hope and Mrs. Marksman again." I looked around and spotted a clock radio on the bedside table. "Well, Mr. Marksman, I have to be going. I have to sign some papers with your lawyer, then I'm catching a flight home. My little girl is four, and she misses her mommy."

He reached over and took my hand. "Can't you sit with me for a few more minutes? I'd like to talk about a few things before you go."

I sighed. "All right, just a few more minutes." I gently pulled my hand away and sat, facing him, on the chair near the wall.

At first he told me about the years in Graytown since my family moved away, as if I had any interest at all in the new traffic light on Cedar Street, or the trees damaged in that big nor'easter, or the big sale when the old pharmacy closed down. I nodded politely and made appropriate noises of approval or concern.

Every now and then, he would say something that made no sense at all. Then he would catch himself, close his eyes for a few seconds to shake off the effects of all the morphine, and go on with his story.

I was just beginning to squirm in my chair, when he lifted his head off the pillow and fixed me with those eyes. "Have you seen Hope in that house, wearing that darn white confirmation dress that Gloria made for her? It's all she ever wears any more. Does she ever speak or smile to you?"

I wasn't sure how to respond. "I remember the white dress she wore to her confirmation. There was a picture of her in it on the mantel."

He stared at the ceiling. "You know, in all the years I lived alone in that house, she never spoke a single damn word to me, or smiled. But she was there all the same. Her and those eyes. I finally had to get the hell out of there."

"Um, I'm sorry the picture made you so sad," I said. "I... I know Hope loved you."

"It should have been me that died, you know. Not Hope. She was pure and clean, and hell, that's the opposite of me." He hesitated for a few seconds. "I thought booze would help, but the more I drank, the more I saw her in that damned white dress."

He closed his eyes again and lay there motionless. Silently praying that he had fallen asleep, I stood up to see if I could sneak out of the room.

I was nearly to the door when I heard him laugh. I turned back, and he looked straight into my soul. "Now," he said softly, "you can become Hope's prisoner."

Still staring at me, he pushed the morphine button one more time, then turned to face away from me.

I spent the next two hours in the hospital cafeteria with Mr. Smith, going over and signing papers that I didn't completely understand. When we finished, I decided that I had plenty of time to say goodbye to your father before heading to the airport.

Just outside the door to his room, Nurse Linzi stopped me. "Mr. Marksman is in a coma," she said. The doctors are looking at him right now, so it will be a few minutes before you can see him. If you'll wait in the lounge down the hall, I'll come get you when they're done."

Mr. Smith was already sitting in the waiting room. I sat down in the chair next to him and said, "I feel like I'm a horrible person for even asking, but if Mr. Marksman doesn't wake up, have I honored his final wishes?"

"Yes, dear, you have," he replied. He reached over and squeezed my hand, then sat back in his chair.

We sat there quietly until the nurse poked her head around the corner. "You can see him now," she said. "I'm afraid he won't know you're there, though."

Mr. Smith followed me into your father's room, then stood by the window while I went over to the bed. I took your father's right hand in mine, surprised by the tears that were welling up in my eyes. I stood there for a few minutes, thinking how fragile he looked, then I leaned over and gave him a kiss on his forehead. "You were like a father to me once," I said. "I did love you then. Thank you."

I released his hand and looked back to thank Mr. Smith. Before I could speak, a white moth fluttered up from one of the fake daisies, flew across the room, and out the door.

Your father never woke up from his coma, and back in Concord, NH eleven days, later I got the call from Mr. Smith that Damian Marksman had died. Strange, I thought, that you died at age eleven, and your father died eleven days after slipping into a coma. According to Mr. Smith, he'd even taken his final breath at almost the exact time of day that his daughter had taken hers.

It took some time for me to convince Nick that accepting your father's gift would be the right thing to do. It was helpful that Nick had a job offer from a company in Boston, which was a short commute from Graytown. And the advantages of living rent-free were compelling. Besides, the house was beautiful, and we were both excited at the idea of choosing paint colors, laying new carpet, and all the other things that would make it our home.

We decided to try the house in Graytown for a year. Then, if we were not happy, we could sell it and go anywhere we chose.

When my parents heard about my unexpected inheritance, they advised us to sell the house and buy one near them in Derry, NH. They felt that it was not healthy for me to move back to Graytown, never mind living in your house. In the end, though, Nick and I decided to give it a try.

As your father's executor, I had to make a special trip to Graytown to meet with Mr. Smith and sign off on all the preparations for his burial. He had left instructions that he was to be cremated and his ashes flown back to Graytown, to be buried next to you and your mother in Ansel Cemetery.

I had expected to simply fill out more paperwork at Mr. Smith's office, but when we were finished, Mr. Smith handed me an envelope.

"Mr. Smith, I'm confused. What's this, please?" I asked.

"Mrs. Rhodes, Mr. Marksman asked that this envelope be handed to you after he died. Truthfully, I have no idea what's in it."

I opened the envelope and dumped a small key into my hand. "What is this?" I asked.

Mr. Smith peered at the key through his round bifocal glasses. "Perhaps there is some sort of explanatory note?"

I shook the envelope over the desk and felt around inside. "No note," I said.

"And the key means nothing to you, Mrs. Rhodes?"

"No, it doesn't," I said. "I don't believe I've ever seen it before. Do you think it might go to a safety deposit box, or P.O. Box, or something?"

"I can certainly check for you and see if there's anything in our records that I might have missed."

"Thank you," I said, and stashed the key in a zippered pocket inside my purse.

A week later I received a note from Mr. Smith that he had not found any record of an unaccounted-for lockbox or anything else in Damian Marksman's name that would explain the mysterious key.

Later, while I was moving my things into the kitchen at the Graze Street house, the old pottery jar your mother kept on top of the refrigerator caught my eye. We kids called it the "honey pot," in tribute to Winnie the Pooh and the fact that on special occasions your mother would let us fish in that jar for pennies when we were very young.

All these years later the jar was empty, and as I turned it over in my hands my mind wandered back to when you and I were very young. The neck of the jar was fairly narrow, with no room for a fist full of coins to get out. The trick was to not get greedy, to take only as many coins as you could without getting your hand stuck.

The last time you and I went for coins in the jar, my hand was bigger than yours, so I could only get a few coins. With your smaller hand, you were able to pull out two more. When I complained that my fat fingers were keeping me poor, you just smiled and handed me one of your extra coins.

Thinking back on your generosity, I knew that the honey pot would be the perfect place to store the key.

As I dropped the key in the empty jar, I recalled one of my favorite quotes from Winnie the Pooh, "If there ever comes a day when we can't be together, keep me in your heart, I'll stay there forever."

Ansel

Engraved granite archways overhead loom
Leaves on two watchful oak trees still bloom
A protective helmet placed divinely by Him
On believers residing here now absent of sin
The earthly body only, entombed in a wooden case
As those left, find comfort in scriptures of His grace

Chapter III

I felt like I was losing my mind.

I sat at the kitchen table with my head buried in my arms, sobbing uncontrollably. Part of me knew that casual chats with the ghost of a childhood friend are anything but healthy, while another part of me actually looked forward to your visits. And flowing through it all was that ever-present, crushing, stifling guilt.

I could almost feel the gloating of the oak tree in the yard, as if it somehow felt my despair and found pleasure in it. It was mocking me, challenging me to water its roots with my tears, just as I'd done so many years ago. But I denied that tree, keeping my distance and even avoiding looking at it directly. I certainly didn't have any desire to hang from the branches anymore, the way you and I once did.

Oh, but we did have fun on the old tire swing, back when we were very young. We sat on top of the tire, imagining that the stick jammed through the rope was the control yoke of our airplane, borne aloft by the oak tree, and taking turns as the pilot soaring through the skies.

By the time we were about nine or ten, we had grown tired of our little airplane, and the rope was frayed to the point of breaking. We barely noticed when your father cut it down, leaving behind the deep divot where the rope had grown into the branch. That divot was the only remaining trace of the hours you and I spent swinging and climbing in the branches of that tree.

Then there were the endless afternoons we sat with our backs against its bark, talking and daydreaming. The old tree knew all our dreams, fears, and secrets. It knew us wearing mittens, gloves, hats, scarves, shorts, bathing suits, long shirts, t-shirts, Easter dresses, sneakers, flip-flops, and even bare feet. It saw us enjoying hot cocoa, water bottles, juice bottles, and popsicles.

And now that tree was the enemy, standing in the yard and silently mocking me.

Then I found myself walking out onto the porch, not bothering to grab a jacket or even to close the door behind me, and crossing the lawn in the cool evening air to stand at the base of the oak tree. I clenched my fists to set my courage, and looked directly at it for the first time in a very long time. "All right tree," I snarled, "Just to be clear, I can cut you down any damn time I want to." I stood there for a few moments, trembling with rage.

Then I felt the anger drain away, washed out by an overwhelming sadness, and I began to cry again, shaking with sobs of grief, and loneliness, and regret. And, ultimately, with sobs of relief. I felt your presence, off to my left, and turned to look.

There sat my boat, the *Afta-U*, resting on its metal blocks. I stared at it while the tears dried on my cheeks. Of course you were there, in that boat that was, after all, named after you.

I heard Nick calling my name and tried to wipe my eyes with the palms of my hands. I realized that I was shivering with cold. "Oh, hi honey," I said, as casually as I could manage.

"I've been calling you," he said. "What are you doing out here?"

"I'm sorry, I was deep in thought," I said.

"What's wrong? Is Meg alright? Has something happened to your parents?"

"No, everything's fine." I shivered again.

"You're freezing," he said. "Here, take my jacket." He wrapped his suit coat around my shoulders, then rubbed his hands up and down my arms. "Why are you crying?" he asked.

I turned back to face the oak tree. "I don't even know where to start. I guess it's time you knew the whole story about that horrible day."

"The story about your friend? About Hope?"

"About Hope. This is where it happened."

"Oh."

We were eleven years old.

It was a brisk fall day, and five of us were just hanging out. I was wearing my grey hooded sweatshirt, the one with the picture of a gorgeous Morgan horse on it, and old hand-me-down jeans with the legs rolled up at the ankles. It bothered me to have them rolled up because it made me feel off-center, but I had no choice because the legs were too long. On my feet were the bright white Keds sneakers I'd grabbed off the laundry line in the cellar. They had just been washed, and I could still smell the bleach.

Hope had on her light yellow jacket with the green butterfly embroidered on the chest. The hood was tucked and zipped, and the sleeves, like my jeans, had to be rolled up. Her brand-new jeans fit her perfectly, though. I knew that inside her jacket, her jeans, and every other article of clothing she owned, her mother had written her name in perfect penmanship with a permanent marker.

On our wrists Hope and I wore the carefully-beaded friendship bracelets that we'd made for each other.

Hope's mother was inside the house cleaning, playing an ABBA record loud enough to hear over the vacuum cleaner and nearly drown out the songs of the birds outside. Michael, Katie, Danny, Hope, and I were sitting under the oak tree, bored and aimless, trying to decide on something we all wanted to do.

It was Michael who had the brainstorm. "Let's play the 'Fainting Game,'" he said.

The rest of us were reluctant. We had seen Gerry and Gary, two of the older kids, play this "game" once. Gerry had stood with his back against a tree while Gary held one hand over Gerry's mouth and pinched his nose with the other hand. After a few moments, Gerry passed out. A minute or two later Gerry woke up laughing, and the two traded roles. The idea was that when you passed out, you got a sort of high, almost as if you were on drugs.

A few of our friends had tried it since, including Michael, but the rest of us had only watched. It had always seemed dangerous to me, and I was petrified to try it. No one listened to my objections or suggestions for other games to play, though, so Michael went first.

He leaned against the tree and said, "Come on Danny, get over here and do it. I want my fix."

"That's not funny, Michael," said Katie. "My dad had a drug problem."

"Well, he should've tried this instead," Michael replied.

"All right then, just shut him up, Danny," said Katie.

Danny nervously covered Michael's mouth and nose, turned his head to the side, and closed his eyes until Michael's body relaxed and he slid down the tree unconscious. We all stood silently looking at Michael, and I found myself thinking, Please wake up. Please God, please wake him up.

After what seemed like an eternity, Michael gasped, opened his eyes, and laughed. "Wow, that was awesome! Okay, Danny, you're next."

I can still see the look of perverse joy on Michael's face as Danny's eyes rolled back in his head and he went limp. He seemed to be getting a real pleasure out of stopping his friend's breathing. Out of the corner of my eye, I could see Hope holding a leaf by its stem and absently twirling it around as she watched. Danny writhed around on the ground for a bit, almost as if he was having a small seizure, just before he regained consciousness.

Once he recovered, Danny jumped to his feet and acted exhilarated by the experience. "You're not kidding! That was awesome!" he said.

Hope went next, then Katie, and each time I watched and prayed, willing them to wake up.

Then it was my turn, and Hope encouraged me. "You have to try it, Jean. It's an absolute rush. Words can't describe it!"

I leaned my back against the oak tree, but as Michael reached out to cover my mouth, I panicked and lunged away, knocking him off his feet. I could hear everyone else laughing, with Michael lying on his back, shouting, "Chicken!"

Hope interrupted them. "Stop it! Just stop it! She's scared, that's all." She smiled and gave my hand a little squeeze. "It's okay, Jean. I'll show you. I'll take your place and go again." Then she smiled, closed her eyes, and leaned back against the tree.

After just a few seconds her eyes flew open and she began flailing her arms. Michael just kept that grin on his face and held on tighter. I began crying and pleading, "Stop! Please stop! She wants you to stop!"

But Michael didn't stop. In fact one of the rules of the Fainting Game is that you never stop until they faint, so nobody moved in to interfere.

When Hope stopped struggling, Michael released her and she collapsed on the ground, where she lay gurgling. Her eyes were open and rolled back in her head. I dropped to my knees next to her. "Come on Hope, wake up." I began to shake her by the shoulders. "Wake up! Please Hope! Please God, wake her up! Come on Hope, please!" I was sobbing hard, my tears falling on that green butterfly on her jacket.

Then she stopped gurgling, and I spotted blood coming out of her ear. I sat back on my heels, while Katie got down on one knee next to Hope and felt for a pulse. "You guys, she's not breathing. I think she might be dead," said Katie.

We all just sat there and nobody said anything. The only sound was the hum of the vacuum cleaner and the music from the house:
Honey I'm still free,
Take a chance on me...

"Jean, you can't blame yourself," Nick said.

"Nick, wait, please don't say anything yet. There's more to the story." I could feel the color draining from my face.

"More? Okay, I'm listening."

While Katie, Danny and I all stared at Hope, helpless, Michael walked over to the garden and returned with a large rock in his hand. Then, without a word, he raised it over his head and smashed it into the center of Hope's forehead. Blood splattered everywhere, hitting my arm and cheek. I froze, my mouth open, trying to find some sense in what Michael had just done.

He dropped the rock on the ground, then rolled Hope over so that her forehead lay on top of it. When he looked up, there was an almost inhuman look in his eyes. "It was an accident," he said. "Hope slipped and hit her head on this rock. That's the story we are all going to tell. Got it?" We all stood silently for another few seconds.

Then I felt like I'd been slapped awake. "Mrs. Marksman!" I screamed, and ran into the house.

When the police arrived, Michael tried to tell his story, but I don't think they believed him for even a second. Finally, I couldn't stand it any longer. "Michael's lying," I sobbed. "He did it! He killed her!"

Mrs. Marksman stared at Michael, her mouth opening and closing as if she were trying to form words. Then the words came:

"What did you do? My baby, what did you do to her?"Two officers had to restrain her while a detective put handcuffs on Michael.

Later, as they led Michael away to the squad car, he locked eyes with me. I was terrified by the look on his face. He showed no fear, no remorse, just a cold, calm, pure excitement.

"It was that look in Michael's eyes that really stuck with me. I started having nightmares almost right away. Those eyes..."

"Honey, a day like that would give anybody nightmares." Nick kissed me on the cheek and gently brushed a few stray strands of hair from my face.

"After a while, the nightmares changed. I would be watching Hope, and then I was Hope, struggling for air, fighting to breathe. Then I'd dream about choking on things. Pills."

"Choking on pills. Wow, now I get the whole pill thing. So what happened to Michael?"

"The next day a detective came to the house. She spent a lot of time asking for details about everything Michael did, and she was really patient with me when I broke down. She told me that later I might have to tell it all again in court."

"It sounds like they were being sensitive to a traumatized child."

"I guess. Then a few weeks went by, and nothing happened."

"It all takes time."

"No, that's not it. I mean, nothing happened. After all those weeks my mother sat me down and told me that there was not going to be any kind of public trial."

"What?"

"She said that I was not going to have to go to court to testify against Michael, that they had settled the whole thing between the judge, Hope's family, and Michael's family. She said that Michael was going to a children's psychiatric facility, and that I was never to discuss it again."

"Wow, I can't imagine being in the Marksman's shoes." Nick shook his head. "I just can't see myself agreeing to something like that."

"I couldn't either. I was really angry that he wasn't going to pay for what he did."

"I don't blame you."

"Within a few months, Michael's parents, Marilyn and Joseph Grainger, moved away from town, before they even sold their house."

"And you were never allowed to talk about any of this?"

"My parents did send me to counseling. I just told the therapists how much I missed Hope and that I was finding a way to move on without her. I never told them that it was all my fault."

"Wait, what? How was it your fault? Nobody could blame you for what happened."

"Nick, there were so many things I should have done. I could have stopped the whole horrible game. I could have taken my turn." I was starting to cry again. "It should have been me. Oh God, Hope..."

My knees gave out, but Nick caught me and held me close in his arms. We stood there for a long time with me sobbing into Nick's chest while he held me and stroked my hair. Finally, he kissed me on the forehead and said, "Feel better now?"

I sniffed and wiped my eyes with the back of my hand. "A little."

"I'm glad you finally got that off your chest."

"You're the only person I've told the whole story to. I also have a confession to make. About the boat."

"Ok, while we're confessing."

"I called the boat *Afta-U* as a way of naming it for Hope Marksman. All these years I've had trouble saying or even thinking of her name, and this was my way of getting around that."

Nick looked over my shoulder at the boat and chuckled. "Meg thinks it's about her."

"I know," I said. "Don't break her heart."

"My lips are sealed," he said.

I pushed back a little and looked into his eyes. "You love me, right?" I asked.

"That's a silly question. Of course I do."

"Unconditionally?"

"Unconditionally."

I sighed. "There's one more thing."

Nick studied my face. "Go on."

"Hope has been visiting me."

"Excuse me?"

"For the past few months, her ghost has been coming to see me."

"Her... ghost."

"Nick, I'm not crazy. OK, maybe I am. I don't know. But she comes to see me almost every day. When she's here, I see her as plainly as I see you right now."

"Is she here right now?"

"No, of course not."

"Wow. Ok, this is going to take some thought. Honey, don't take this the wrong way, but maybe we need to work on getting you some help."

"So you think I'm crazy?"

"I didn't say that. Jean, you've been through an unbelievable trauma. For all these years, you've blamed yourself for a tragedy you couldn't have changed. Baby, nobody can deal with something like that without professional help."

"So you're sticking with that unconditional love thing?"

"Absolutely."

"Thank goodness."

"Jean, I love you. We'll get through whatever this is as a family."

That night, and for the next few nights, I dreamt of my grandfather's sailboat. I could still smell the fresh blue paint on the rowboat as my grandfather, my mother, and I rowed out to the Flying Scot to take her for a sail. It was a beautiful day, and the skies were clear.

Then, without any warning, the boat capsized, and I was bobbing around in my child-sized orange life vest, screaming and taking in mouthfuls of salt water. I couldn't see my grandfather or mother anywhere. All I could think of was that they were trapped under the capsized boat, and that I was helpless to save them. Or myself.

I never woke Nick up, but this exact dream came back night after night.

The funny thing is, rowing out to the Flying Scot with my mother and grandfather in the freshly painted blue rowboat actually happened. Of course, in real life, the boat never capsized. It was the same weekend I stepped on a crab and also on a fishing hook. I lost hours I could have spent in the ocean going to the hospital to have the hook removed and get a tetanus booster.

The really strange aspect of that dream is the idea that I should be afraid of the water. But I wasn't. I spent my childhood swimming in the ocean, in lakes, and in pools. I was on the swim team. And I spent some of the happiest hours of my life sailing, never afraid of capsizing or falling in. There was even a time when I thought that I would live on a boat and sail it all around the world.

This all changed over the years. Besides cutting up pills, I found that I was nervous in a swimming pool, and could only hold my breath underwater for a few seconds at a time – a big change from a girl who was once proud that she could swim whole laps underwater on a single breath.

The office was the last room in the house left to renovate. It was my sanctuary, the one place I could come to block out the rest of the world and write my third novel. I'd chosen a neutral tan for the walls, and ivory for around the chair rail and wooden trim. I was having hardwood floors refinished to their original, natural state.

Before we could paint, I had to pack away all the books and knick-knacks from the built-in bookcases that filled one entire wall of the office. I fondly picked up a snow globe, a gift from an old college friend, and made it snow on the golden retriever inside, chasing her puppies around an oak tree. When I turned to put the snow globe in the bin, it slipped out of my hand and smashed on the floor.

Upset, I grabbed a broom, tray, trash bag, and a roll of paper towels from the storage closet to clean up the mess.

As I carefully picked up some of the larger pieces of glass, I noticed that the floorboard closest to the corner of the wall was lifted up slightly, and water from the snow globe was flowing down the crack.

I leaned down to take a closer look, picking up a sliver of glass in the palm of my left hand. I was in the bathroom with a pair of tweezers and a tube of Neosporin when I heard the garage door opening.

A few minutes later, Nick was in the bathroom doorway. "Do I dare ask what you did?" he asked.

"It was just me being clumsy. Would you check my hand to see if there is any more glass?"

Nick gently took my hand in his and moved closer to the light from the window. "Nope, looks like you got it. So now, what's the story?"

"Honestly, I wish it was a good one," I laughed. "I dropped a snow globe on the floor in the office."

"So, one less piece of junk to pack."

I punched him in the shoulder. "Ellen gave it to me. I liked it."

Back in the office, Nick was holding the dustpan for me when I said, "By the way, there is a board sticking up in the corner there. Make sure you tell the guys doing the floors to take care of it."

He poked at the board with his thumb. "I think it's loose. I'll grab the pry bar out of the garage and see what it'll take to fix it."

When Nick pried the corner of the board, it popped right up, along with the two adjacent boards. There, in a space beneath the floor, sat a fireproof metal box.

"Well, there's something you don't see every day," said Nick. He pulled the box out and shook it. "It's been there for years. I hope it's full of cash."

I gulped hard. "I don't think it's cash."

"If only we had the key," he said. "Good thing we have a pry bar."

"We won't need it." I was having trouble catching my breath. "Bring the box and come on."

Nick followed me into the kitchen. I dragged a chair over to the refrigerator, took down the honey pot, and dumped the key onto the table.

"Where'd you get that?" asked Nick.

"It's the last thing Damian Marksman left for me." With shaking hands I put the key in the keyhole and turned it. The lock opened with a click.

The box contained three sheets of paper, each neatly folded in half. I picked up the one on top and opened it. It was a birth certificate, and I caught my breath as I read the name on it: Michael Paul Grainger. It listed Michael's mother as Marilyn Grainger, but the birth father as "Unknown."

I handed the birth certificate to Nick and unfolded the next document. It was from a clinical laboratory, reporting on the blood types of the Grainger family. Joseph Grainger was type AB, and Marilyn Grainger was type A. My heart sank as I read that Michael was type O. Across the bottom of the report was a handwritten note from the laboratory, that Joseph Grainger could not possibly be Michael's biological father.

The next page was a paternity test, dated two days after Hope's death. It named Damian Marksman as Michael Grainger's biological father. For a few seconds, I thought I was going to be sick.

I swallowed hard and handed the report to Nick, then picked up the last item in the box. It was a photograph of a young woman standing next to a battered red pickup truck. She wore a long brown coat and a short brown skirt, with a cream-colored top and brown heels. She held her hands over her face to block the camera. I recognized the truck as Damian Marksman's.

I flipped the picture over to look for a date. Whatever had been written on the back of the picture had been carefully and completely blackened out in pen.

"Well, now we know why they sent Michael away," said Nick.

I looked up from the photo. "Yes, I guess we do. Look at this." I handed him the photo. "That's Damian's truck, and I think the woman is Marilyn Grainger."

Then I felt my composure crack, and I burst into tears. I slumped into my husband's arms and cried.

The next morning as I sat across the kitchen table from you with my morning coffee, I couldn't stop thinking about the contents of that lockbox. Nick was right; it was obvious why your parents settled for sending Michael to the psychiatric hospital, but I couldn't understand why your mother didn't just leave as soon as she learned the truth about Michael.

And that photograph. It might have been taken the very night Michael was conceived. I thought back to your father's deathbed rant: *"You just had to insist on stretching things further. It was the night after that argument that he happened. You forced me to leave for the night, remember? Future planning, all right, godammit! Well, that worked out perfectly now, didn't it?"*

It all made sense. You and Michael are the same age, so Gloria must have been pregnant with you when they had some sort of fight over setting up the college fund for their unborn child. What I couldn't understand is where I fit in, why your father left everything to me. Was he trying to punish me? I could feel the anger welling up in me. "Your father was one hell of a son of a bitch!" I yelled at you. Of course, you never flinched.

And I thought about that moth in his hospital room. Did you send it to me as some sort of sign or warning? He left me that key with no other information, knowing that I might never find the box and learn the truth. What sort of game was he playing?

I pictured Michael rotting away in some psychiatric facility, a forty-year-old man, maybe sitting in a beige room playing checkers with some other hopeless patient. Had anyone ever bothered to tell him that the girl he killed was not only his friend, she was his half-sister?

The Old Oak Tree

The whispering branches and colored dropping leaves
Speak a foreign language in the breeze
The howling wind she creates screams
Somehow, entrapping both my nightmares and dreams
Distorting her bark wrinkles that mask her true age
Envisioning a dead parakeet now uncaged
Grasping with gripped ghostly claws
The strongest arm tested with a few divot flaws
A wiser witness to that dreaded day
That took Hope, along with childhood innocence, away

Chapter IV

I have always loved the newspaper. Every morning I fetch it from the front porch while the coffee is brewing, then sit at the table to read it from cover to cover. I even love the smell of the newsprint, and the faint aroma it leaves on my hands.

So sitting at the table that morning with you silently next to me as I flipped through the pages, I felt calm and even happy. I had two hours until my appointment with my new therapist, Dr. Grant.

When I reached the obituary section, my eyes fell on a familiar name halfway down the page:

> Cassie Kiter Bellows. Loved and missed by her family and friends. Interment to be held Thursday, September 28, at Ansel Cemetery, Graytown, MA, including a brief service by Father Edward Stacy Adams from St. John's Church, High Street, Graytown, MA. In lieu of flowers, please send donations to The Lance House, P. O. Box 603, Riverdale, MA, 04561.

I stared at the obituary and read it again. I felt ashamed at the slight surge of relief I felt in reading about the passing of Mrs. Bellows, a woman I'd known nearly all my life. Maybe it was the thought that your mother's letter might be buried forever with this woman who had been both my enemy and my ally. Had she read it? Destroyed it?

I decided that I had to go to her funeral. A few days later, driving through the granite archway entrance to Ansel Cemetery, something Margaret Thatcher once said popped into my mind: "It pays to know the enemy, not least because at some time you may have the opportunity to turn him into a friend."

I parked at the end of the small line of cars near the grave site. As I turned off the car engine, I repeated a mantra; "This is a serene resting place filled with love. This is a serene resting place filled with love." The mourners were gathered just up the hill, to the left of your family's graves. *This is a serene resting place filled with love.*

I opened the door and stepped out of the car.

There were around thirty people standing around or sitting in the row of chairs, waiting for the service to begin. I was proud of myself for attending without Nick, who had an important meeting. I still hadn't told him the details about your mother's death, or about the letter and Mrs. Bellows' relationship to it all. I had simply told him I was attending the funeral of a woman I had known since childhood.

As I scanned the crowd of mourners, my heart nearly stopped when I saw a startlingly familiar pair of deep blue eyes staring back at me. Despite all the years that has passed, there was no mistaking Michael Grainger and those eyes – your eyes, and your father's eyes.

His father's eyes.

Michael had grown up to be the image of Damian Marksman, with the same sharp, handsome face and athletic body. He was dressed in a dark suit and tie, and had his hair lightly gelled and brushed back, revealing a bit of a receding hairline. He had a very trendy carefully-tended five-day scruffy beard, and only the faint wrinkles around his eyes gave away his actual age.

Even from a distance his eyes seemed to stare right through me. I wondered if he had any idea how terrified I was to see him again.

He was standing next to a tall, slender, beautiful young woman with dark skin and piercing green eyes, and the sunlight streaming through the trees reflected off the gold wedding band on his left hand.

Next to the young woman sat Mrs. Bellows' daughter, Isabella, who was clearly having trouble controlling her grief. Her wails of pure heartbreak were keeping the ceremony from beginning. I wondered if she had been away from the assisted living facility and living with Mrs. Bellows when the end came.

The young woman leaned down and embraced Isabella, stroking her long, dark hair, which calmed Isabella down enough for the service to begin. When the young woman straightened up, still holding Isabella's hand to comfort her, I could see that tears were streaming down her face. I wondered if she was a relative of Mrs. Bellows, or just an empathetic nurse taking care of Isabella.

All this time Michael stood staring directly at me. Without breaking his gaze, he reached down and took the young woman's free hand, giving it a tender squeeze.

I was totally distracted by all this, so I missed hearing most of Father Adams' eulogy and sermon. Still in a daze, I watched Isabella, Michael, and the young woman step up to the grave and each lay a red rose on top of the casket, a ritual normally reserved for only the closest of family members. But how was Michael connected to Mrs. Bellows?

It crossed my mind that if Mrs. Bellows had read your mother's letter, she would know the truth about Michael – information I felt certain was in that envelope. Maybe she never read it, and simply destroyed it. It was the only way I could explain Michael somehow becoming an intimate part of the Bellows family.

For a moment I was relieved that the letter may indeed have been destroyed, and then I felt a flush of panic and guilt at the thought that if Mrs. Bellows had known the truth about Michael, she would never have let a monster like him become an intimate part of her life.

I took a deep breath and brought back my mantra – *This is a serene resting place filled with love* – silently repeating it all the way back to my car. I was still sitting behind the wheel, trying to calm myself with my mini-meditation and waiting for the traffic to clear, when I was startled by a knock on the car window.

It was Mr. Smith, your father's lawyer. He had aged a lot since the last time I saw him, and had to be at least seventy-five years old. I opened the window and worked up a friendly smile. "Hello, Mr. Smith."

"Hello, Mrs. Rhodes. I was not sure you would recognize me. It's been a very long time."

"Of course I recognize you. How have you been?"

"Getting older, I'm afraid. I'll be retiring from my practice by the end of the year."

"How nice for you. Do you and Mrs. Smith have any exciting retirement plans?"

"Nancy just got out of the hospital, I'm afraid. Nothing terribly serious, but we are taking our time with that sort of planning."

"I'm so glad she's feeling better. Well, it looks like the traffic is starting to move. It was wonderful seeing you again Mr. Smith. Please give my regards to Nancy."

Mr. Smith glanced up at the traffic then back to me. "Thank you for the kind wishes, Mrs. Rhodes, and this has been a pleasant chat, but I also have some business we need to attend to. I'll be brief." He handed me his business card. "I assume you remember where my office is."

"Of course."

"You are invited to the reading of Cassie Bellows' will, this Friday morning at 10 a.m." He must have seen the color drain from my face, because he went on, "Oh please don't worry! Mrs. Bellows simply had something she was keeping for you, and her will stipulated that I turn it over to you at the reading."

"The reading is Friday? Is there a way I can pick it up beforehand?"

"I'm afraid that's not possible. It's just the way these things work. I could arrange to have you pick it up after the reading."

The driver of the car behind me in line, just polite enough to refrain from honking the horn in a cemetery, revved his engine. "Oh dear," said Mr. Smith, "we are holding up traffic. You have my number. Please call my office. Good-bye, Mrs. Rhodes. And God bless."

I drove home on autopilot. It just had to be that letter; there was nothing else Mrs. Bellows could be "keeping for me." Since Michael was around, maybe she hadn't read it. Or maybe it didn't contain the information I thought it did. Or maybe... the possibilities were dizzying. The only thing I knew for certain is that I would only have a few more days to wait for the answers. If I even wanted the answers. Maybe I would simply burn it without reading it, and finish what I'd started all those years ago.

An angel must have been watching over me, because somehow I got home safely.

I decided that a warm shower would help me relax. I stood under the showerhead and allowed the water to flow over me for what seemed like forever. Then I wrapped myself up in an extra-large white towel and picked out the most comfortable outfit I could find.

Dressed and back downstairs, I dug Mr. Smith's business card out of my purse and called the number.

"Smith Law Office, this is Mary, how may I help you?"

"Yes, Mary, this is Jean Rhodes. Mr. Smith asked me to call and schedule an appointment concerning something left for me from the estate of Cassie Bellows," I said.

"Why yes, Mrs. Rhodes. Can you attend the reading of the will on Friday?"

"I'm not family, so I'm afraid it might be awkward."

"Mrs. Bellows wanted her friends as well as family to gather together for the reading, but I do understand. If you're unable to attend, we can schedule a meeting next week with Mr. Smith."

"What about Friday after the reading?"

"I'm afraid Mr. Smith's schedule is full all day Friday, and he's in court Monday. We could set up something for Tuesday."

I choked back tears, wavering between the dread of attending the reading of another will, and the thought of waiting through a long weekend for some sort of resolution. I cleared my throat and composed myself. "No, thanks, Mary. I'll be there for the reading. Friday at 10."

"Very well, Mrs. Rhodes. I'll let Mr. Smith know. Good-bye."

Time is both an ally and a foe to all of God's creatures. At this particular point in my life, time was slowly beating me down.

My anxiety over the meeting was just too powerful for me to hide from Nick. When he got home that evening, he knew something was wrong. He kissed me hello and said, "All right. What's wrong?"

I broke down and began to cry. "I'm sorry I didn't tell you the whole story," I said.

"What story?" Nick asked.

"About what happened after Hope died."

Nick pulled out a chair and sat across the table from me, then reached across and took both of my shaking hands in his. "Ok, let's hear it."

"The woman whose funeral I just attended, Cassie Bellows, was more than just someone I knew as a child." I went on to tell Nick the entire story about your mother's death, about the letter, and about my trip to Dead Man's Peak. I told him about my fear of what was in the letter, and about Mrs. Bellows' part in all of it. And I told him about the reading of the will on Friday.

Nick gave my hands a squeeze. "Maybe it's not 'the letter.' Maybe it's a letter telling you that she destroyed Hope's mom's letter. Maybe it's an envelope full of ashes. Or maybe she turned it over to the authorities years ago without telling them about your part in it, and whatever they have for you is something completely different."

"I don't know. Maybe."

"I really don't understand why you tried burn to the envelope in the first place."

"I guess I thought I was protecting Hope and her mother. I didn't want people to look down on them. Then it all got complicated."

"Well it's just about over now. If you get the letter back you can do what you want with it, and then we can put all this behind us."

"But there's another thing – Michael Grainger was at the funeral today."

"Seriously?"

"Yes. I always assumed that he would spend the rest of his life locked away somewhere, but he was there. And he is somehow very close to Mrs. Bellows' family."

"That's very strange," said Nick. "If we assume there is something in Mrs. Marksman's letter about who Michael's father is, then..."

"Then if she didn't read the letter, Mrs. Bellows didn't have fair warning what kind of person she was letting close to her. Another thing that I can blame myself for."

"It is not your fault." Nick lifted my hands and kissed them. "None of this is your fault. You have to believe that."

"Nick, Michael is going to be at the reading of Mrs. Bellows' will. I don't know if I can be in the same room with him."

"Jean, your anger toward Michael, and all this guilt you're holding inside you has me worried. Have you discussed all this with your therapist? Does she know about the letter?"

I could see the concern in Nick's eyes. "Most of it. But I'm afraid if I tell Dr. Grant about taking the letter from the scene of a death, she would have to tell the police."

"I don't think she can, not unless someone's life is at stake. A therapist is supposed to respect your confidentiality. Besides, this all happened when you were eleven years old. Who would charge you with anything after all these years?"

"I pray that's true. I can't live with all this worry."

"Hasn't Dr. Grant given you something to calm you down?"

"I have a few prescriptions, but I haven't filled them. I'm afraid they'll affect my concentration."

"Under the circumstances, I think they might actually help your concentration. After all you've gone through, you should have been getting help years ago."

"Okay. I'll get them filled today," I said.

Nick smiled, pulled me to my feet and wrapped his arms around me. "Let's go and fill them right now, and get you feeling better." He kissed me gently on the forehead. I pulled back and looked into his eyes, which gave him the opportunity to move the kisses down to my lips.

On the way to the pharmacy Nick said, "Look, I don't want you to go to that thing Friday alone, and I have a huge meeting Friday morning that I can't change. Call them back and schedule a time for next week."

"No, it's fine," I said. "There will be other people around. And maybe it's time I faced Michael and took back some power I've given him."

"I know you can do it alone, but I rather you didn't."

"Don't worry, I'll be fine. He's just a man. And who knows, maybe he's rehabilitated by now." *Liar, liar your pants are on fire.* I didn't believe a single word I'd just said.

"I can get out of work early Friday after my meeting, so I can be here not long after you get home. We can open the envelope together."

"That sounds perfect."

Mr. Smith's office was where it had been for the past forty-five years, in the center of Graytown. In fact, the businesses in the center of town never seemed to change. When Mr. Smith retired, some lucky business was going to end up with prime real estate.

Dr. Grant had prescribed me some Valium, and it was doing the trick. Whenever I started feeling edgy or out of sorts, I could take one pill and all my worries would dissolve away. When I walked into Mr. Smith's office, I was glad that I had taken one just before I left the house, because the first person I ran into was Michael.

He reached out and grabbed my hand to shake it, and I went along, determined to make meeting him into a passing, formal encounter. But then he held onto my hand a little too long, and a little too tightly. "Hello Michael," I said, trying to pull my hand out of his grasp.

He only gripped my hand tighter, and smiled through clenched teeth. "So nice to see you again, Jean." His voice held that same cutting tone that haunted me for all those years. "Although I admit that I'm surprised that my wife's grandmother has included you in her will."

I finally wiggled my hand free, my palm virtually dripping sweat. I struggled to find something to say as my mind reeled. *Cassie Bellows is his wife's grandmother?*

"I don't know, Jean," continued Michael. "Cassie could be a little bit odd at times. Maybe she left you all her hats."

I managed to regain my composure and said, "Whatever Mrs. Bellows chose to leave for me is a private matter." I tried to dry my hand discretely on my pants. "Did I understand you to say that Cassie Bellows was your wife's grandmother? I didn't realize she had any children other than Isabella."

"You heard right. I married Isabella's daughter," Michael said.

My mind was racing with questions. How could Isabella have conceived a child? Where was she raised, and by whom? The beautiful young woman at the cemetery was obviously Michael's wife, and his relationship with Mrs. Bellows was closer than I could have imagined.

Michael's smile broadened. "It seems like you're surprised to see me, Jean. Don't tell me you thought that they'd leave an eleven-year-old boy locked away forever."

"Yes," I said. "Actually, Michael, I did."

I turned my back on him, trying to look calm as I walked toward a seat across the room. I heard his sadistic laugh behind me.

Before long, Mr. Smith came into the office, gave us all a courteous smile, and opened a brown binder. "Before we begin the reading of Cassie Bellows' last will and testament," he said, "I have been instructed to inform you all that the order of the items detailed herein was carefully determined by Mrs. Bellows, but that it in no way reflects any sort of chronological sequence, or the importance any individual held in her heart."

The Valium I had taken was doing its job, and I felt relatively calm as I waited for Mr. Smith to get around to my part of the will. It turned out that I was last and, ironically, the disposition of Mrs. Bellows' odd collection of hats came just before Mr. Smith said, "Finally, I leave the contents of one manila folder, kept all these years in a safe deposit box, to one Mrs. Jean Cartwright Rhodes. Jean, please do what you think best with its contents."

Mr. Smith handed me the folder, closed the binder, and said "And that concludes the reading of the last will and testament of Mrs. Cassie Kiter Bellows. Good day to you all."

I muttered a quick "thank you" to Mr. Smith and almost ran out of the office, determined to avoid any more conversation with Michael Grainger. In the car on the way home, I tried to think of a new mantra to chant, but all I could think about was that envelope. Part of me wanted to pull off the road, tear it open, and find out exactly what was inside, while another part of me wanted to shred it into a million pieces and never look inside. Instead, I kept driving.

Back home in the garage, I grabbed the envelope off the passenger seat with one hand while I pushed the button on the visor to close the garage door. Out of habit I glanced in the rear view mirror to watch the door closing.

What I saw in the mirror was two young girls, laughing and playing an all-too-familiar game, courting disaster and cheating death by scampering under the closing door at the last possible second.

You were not wearing the white dress I had become accustomed to seeing you in. You and I were both dressed in corduroy pants, rolled at the ankles into big cuffs. Mine were wine colored and yours were black. I had on a paisley, flowered long-sleeved shirt and you were wearing your canary yellow turtleneck. The beaded friendship bracelets were on each of our tiny wrists.

I turned to look over my shoulder, and we were gone.

In the kitchen, I dropped the manila envelope on the table and tossed my black wool pea coat and multi-colored scarf over the back of one of the kitchen chairs. I decided that my mantra while I was waiting for Nick to come home might as well be laundry, so I headed upstairs to the laundry room and loaded the wet clothes from the top-loading washing machine into the dryer, cleaned the lint trap, and added two unscented dryer sheets before turning the dryer on. Finally, I put a white load in to wash and headed back downstairs to stare at the envelope.

I looked up at the clock and realized that I had at least another hour before Nick was likely to get home. I sat there for what seemed like an eternity, rapping my fingers on the table, and it occurred to me that I might be sitting in the exact chair your mother sat in when she wrote the letter.

No, she always sat in the seat nearest the refrigerator, just in case she had to jump up and get something for someone. I got up and moved over to that chair, then picked up the envelope and turned it over in my hands. When I looked back up, I was not the least bit surprised to see you sitting in the chair next to me, back in your white confirmation dress. I showed you the envelope. "What do you think, Hope?" I said. "Let's not wait for Nick to get here. We can take care of this ourselves."

As usual, you just stared back at me.

"Okay then, here's the moment of truth," I said, as I carefully tore open the flap of the envelope, and dumped the contents onto the table.

As I had expected, it was a thick stuffed sealed envelope, with one corner singed. The faded writing on the outside said, "To Whom It May Concern." In addition to this letter, was a single piece of paper which read:

> Dearest Jean,
>
> As you probably know by now, I went back and retrieved this letter you attempted to destroy. I contemplated opening and reading it many times over the years, but it was sealed when you attempted to burn it, and I decided to respect your wishes. On the other hand, I couldn't bring myself to destroy it. You're an adult by now, and you can do what you think best.
>
> I know you didn't write this letter, but I think I have a good idea who did. May God help you in your decision.
>
> Until we meet again,
Best wishes,
Cassie Bellows

With surprisingly steady hands, I opened the envelope and removed the letter. Over time the paper had yellowed, and there was a small singed area on each page, but the writing was still legible. I carefully unfolded the pages and began reading.

> First, let me begin by stating my name is Gloria Minor Marksman. Please accept this letter as both a last will and testament and a final confession.
>
> My daughter, Hope Ann Marksman, was killed during a dangerous game played by a handful of neighborhood children. Please let me state that based on the autopsy

results, I accept her death as a tragic accident. However, upon her death, one Michael Paul Grainger, acting alone, picked up a large rock, smashed the forehead of my daughter, and rolled her over to try to make it appear as though she'd fallen and died from hitting the rock on the ground.

The autopsy results confirmed Hope was dead prior to her skull being smashed by Michael, yet, it disturbs me to my core to think an eleven-year-old boy could act so maliciously. A day after the tragedy, the boy's parents, Mr. Joseph Grainger, Mrs. Marilyn Grainger, and their lawyer approached my husband and me. Our lawyer was called upon to mediate.

We listened as the painful details of one of my husband's indiscretions were revealed. Afterward, tests were conducted which determined that my husband was the biological father of Michael Grainger. The Graingers revealed that Joseph Grainger was impotent and, needless to say, he was aware of his wife's indiscretion immediately after discovering the pregnancy. He forgave his wife and accepted Michael as his own. He even agreed to list Michael's biological father as "unknown" on the boy's birth certificate. We were told that the Graingers had never discussed the truth of Michael's biological father with Michael.

The Graingers reached out to us to beg us to settle in a child's closed court hearing, asking that Michael receive the mental health care he required without the public learning all the details of our situation. Therefore, we all agreed to petition the judge to have Michael placed in a children's sanitarium instead of placing him in juvenile detention.

Michael was placed in the Marblehead Island Sanitarium in the hope that they would be able to rehabilitate him. We were able to keep most of this case out of the local press, and the town gossip almost immediately stopped. After living out this nightmare, I now can understand how some politicians are able to bury some horrific past details within their lives.

Upon hearing this, I'm sure that many people would question why I chose to stay with my husband after Hope's death. There is one really simple answer: I owed him. About four years before I had Hope, when I was nineteen years old, I, too, had an affair. I was only dating my future husband, Damian Marksman, at the time. I told Damian about the affair, and he accepted my remorse, never once questioning whether to stay with me or not. We'd been together since high school, and I want to state for the record, that I did truly love my husband back then.

Shortly after my affair, I found out that I was pregnant. We were never certain if the child was Damian's or this other man's, but Damian decided to stay with me and marry me, on the condition that I give this child up for adoption and never speak of the matter again. He said, "Even if she's mine, she'll have a better life with parents who can provide for her. And if she's not mine, I could never look at her or you without pain and anger."

So we moved away from our home in New England to Rochester, NY, until I gave birth to my healthy daughter, and immediately gave her up for adoption as we'd planned. Damian and I married a month after that.

Not a day has gone by that I don't think of my daughter, and of what she could be doing with her life. To me, she will always be my eldest daughter, Grace Clara Marksman. I had chosen this name just in case Damian changed his mind about the adoption.

The adoption agency we used was Rochester Adoption Resource Exchange located in Rochester, NY, and I gave birth in St. Mary's Hospital, Rochester, NY, with Damian by my side. Today, as I write this letter, it is her birthday. Grace turned sixteen years old at 10:53 a.m.

For my final will and testament, upon my death, I want to ask my husband, Damian Marksman, to close out the bank account we established as a college fund for Hope, and locate my other daughter, Grace, to ensure that this account is available to help her with any future college aspirations. Furthermore, upon the death of my husband, Damian James Marksman, I ask that if he has not remarried, he will please leave our house and any belongings and other assets to Grace Clara Marksman, by whatever adoptive name she may be known. Please make sure that any compensation necessary to locate Grace is paid, and that my husband honors these requests and files all the necessary paperwork.

To ensure his compliance, please have him read this letter.

My dearest Damian, please honor this request as payment for all the years I loved you and stayed with you, despite all your many, many indiscretions throughout our marriage – one of which came back to haunt us both and took the life of our daughter. Please make certain that Grace knows she was always loved by her biological mother.

If her father is not Damian Marksman, then he is one Mark Saga originating from Naples, FL. If Mark is Grace's father, I deeply regret he'll never know that he had a daughter with me. But should Grace ever choose to reach out to the family, please make her aware of the two possible identities of her biological father, by first looking at Damian.

Please, God, forgive me for my sins.

Gloria Minor Marksman

What had I done? The ticking of the kitchen clock grew louder and louder, and I knew that I could do nothing to turn back time to the moment I zipped this letter into the pocket of my blue jacket.

It was obvious no one before me had ever read this letter, or had any idea of its contents other than your mother. I had changed lives by never allowing this letter to be read by the proper authorities.

In fact, I should not have inherited this house! I had kept your father from knowing his wife's final wishes, and he had left it all to me, instead of Grace. If he'd read this letter, he surely would have honored your mother's final wishes. The room was spinning. How was I going to make this all right? My God, was I just as evil as Michael Grainger?

Of course not! How could I possibly have known what was written in this letter? But Michael knew exactly what he was doing when he picked up that rock. Was he only trying to cover up the accident, or had he known on that fateful day that Hope was his half-sister?

My horror at that gruesome thought was almost too much to bear, so I focused my attention on the copper penny stamped with my birth year, a talisman I always carried with me, moving it from my left pants' pocket to my right pants' pocket. It was a calming ritual my therapist had suggested.

And it worked for a few seconds. I put Michael out of my mind and thought about Grace, an almost forty-six-year-old woman, successful and happy. I pictured her having a wonderful, loving childhood with wealthy parents, who sent her to the best schools possible. Maybe she had even become a famous writer, singer, or actor.

But this vision was shattered at the thought that Grace could also be a half-sister to Michael. I moved the penny back again to my left pocket.

I folded and unfolded the letter, trying to wrap my mind around Cassie Bellows' thinking process. Why did she go back to the fire pit to retrieve the letter, then never read it herself? Why didn't she hand it over to the authorities? Could she have been aware of Michael's role in your death? Could she have had any idea that you were Michael's sister? On top of everything else, how could Michael have come to meet Cassie's granddaughter and marry her? How could his life have become so entwined with hers?

While curiosity pulled me toward all these questions, I hoped that I might never cross paths with Michael Grainger again. If it meant keeping Michael out of my life, maybe I could be content not knowing the answer to any of these questions.

But I wasn't completely off the hook. I had tampered with evidence the day of your mother's death, and changed your half-sister's life forever. I had to find Grace and correct this situation, but I wasn't sure how much Nick was going to support me.

I decided that I first needed to reach out to Walter Smith, the only lawyer I really knew and trusted, to get some legal guidance and to ask him to recommend a private investigator who could help me find Grace.

My hands were shaking as I picked up the receiver. The situation felt strangely similar to the night I'd called the ambulance for your mother.

Instead of the white rabbit's foot, I reached into my pocket and took out that faded copper "lucky penny" and rubbed it between the fingers of my free hand. I was actually a little bit relieved to discover that both Mr. Smith and his secretary had left the office. My breathing steadied as I listened to the voice mail message.

I tried to sound calm and business-like. "Mr. Smith, this is Jean Rhodes. I have an urgent matter I need to discuss with you concerning evidence from Mrs. Marksman's death. Can you please call me back as soon as you can, no matter what time it is?"

As I hung up the phone, I heard the buzzer on the clothes dryer go off. I jumped and had to laugh at the idea that my next challenge was folding laundry and trying to match up socks. "Hope, your mom's dryer sock thief has been working overtime lately. Let's see how many are gone from this load. Speaking of socks, do you remember when your mom washed your new black soccer socks with your favorite white shirt?" I laughed a bit louder. "Come on, you have to admit it was funny. When you cried, your

Mom worked her magic and wrote Graytown on it. And then we all wanted one, too."

Suddenly, I stopped laughing. In a way, missing socks, bleeding colors, and Graytown seemed to sum up everything that was going on in my mind.

I sat back down and looked into your expressionless blue eyes. "The day your mother died, she talked to me about free will, you know. She told me that she didn't believe in fate, and I guess I don't either. My 'free will' has made a complete mess of everything. I wish I could just blame it all on 'fate,' and move on."

I was still holding my penny, and I opened my hand to look at it. It was dark and dull, with the lettering and the face of Abraham Lincoln nearly worn away by years of rubbing and riding around in my pockets.

When we were kids, we always flipped my penny to decide who would go first in our games. It was still bright and shiny when we flipped it on that drab, rainy day before you died, when we were about to play "Chinese Jump Rope" in your kitchen. Since there was only two of us, we placed one end under the chair's front legs, and then we just needed to decide who would jump first and who would handle the other end of the rope.

You looked up at the coin tumbling through the air and shouted, "Tails!" On that dreary afternoon of our pure joy together, I don't think it mattered very much to either of us that it turned out to be "heads."

I dropped the penny back into my pocket.

I knew that Nick would be home soon, so I was in the bathroom, rinsing my face and trying to compose myself, when I heard the garage door open. I had just made it back to the kitchen with dry eyes and a forced smile when he walked in. "Hi honey," he said. "How did it go?"

I reached up and gave him a kiss, but as I opened my mouth to speak, I began to cry. All I could do was stand there, opening and closing my mouth and making little gurgling sounds, with tears streaming down my cheeks.

"Baby, here, sit down," Nick said as he guided me into one of the kitchen chairs, sat down next to me, and took my hands in his. He nodded at the letter lying open on the table. "I see you went ahead and opened it. Why didn't you wait for me?"

I sniffed and took a deep breath. "Hope was here. I thought that if she and I read it together, maybe she'd be satisfied and leave."

"Is she still here?"

I looked around the room. "No, she's gone now."

"So was the letter what we thought it was?"

"Yes, and so much more."

"More?"

"Here, it's best if you just read it." I pushed it across the table to him. "I think you'll understand why I already called Mr. Smith and left a message."

Nick picked up the letter and gave me a searching look before he unfolded it and began to read. When he finished, he dropped it on the table and looked back up at me. "Ok, that is a lot to absorb. So what exactly did you call the lawyer about?"

"Nick, if I hadn't tampered with this letter, everything would have gone to Grace. Not me."

"Are you saying that you want to give away our house?" There was a hint of anger in his voice.

"No! That's not what I'm saying." I sat back in my chair and rubbed my eyes with both hands. "Look Nick, I know this letter is not legally binding. Hope's father could have done anything he wanted to do, no matter what her mother wanted. I get that. The house is ours now."

"Then what, exactly, do you have in mind?"

"Gloria wanted Hope's college fund to go to her other daughter, to Grace. Something Damian said in the hospital just before he died makes me believe that the college fund triggered the fight that led to his affair with Mrs. Grainger. And that led to Michael. The thought of that money makes me sick to my stomach."

"So let me get this straight. You want to find a forty-six-year-old woman and give her the money from our daughter's college fund? How does that make any sense at all?"

"Nick, please hear me out. I think I'd like to close out the fund, pay any penalties we have to pay, then give just the amount that Damian left me to Grace. Who knows, maybe she has children who could use it. We can open a new account for Meg with what's left over."

Nick sat silently for a few seconds. "Jean, think about it," he said. "You just found out today that Gloria had another daughter. But Damian Marksman knew all about it when he decided to leave that money to you. What makes you think it would have made any difference at all if he had seen the letter?"

I shook my head. "Don't you see? It doesn't matter what he would or would not have done. This is what I think is right. It's what I want to do, and I need to know that you'll support me."

Nick sat there for what seemed like an eternity, then chuckled gently and shook his head. "One of things I love most about you is your big heart. That money was given to you, and you can give it away if you want to. Especially if it will help you move on with your life."

I moved to sit on his lap, wrapped my arms around his neck and whispered in his ear, "Thank you. Thank you."

He hugged me closer and said, "Everything's going to be all right."

I snuggled into his shoulder and said, "Now I remember why I married you. You're not only big and strong – you're sensitive."

He laughed again. "Look, not to change the subject," he said, "I think you need to talk to Dr. Grant about your meds. If you're still seeing Hope's ghost, they might not be doing their job."

"I'll talk to her."

We were still cuddling when Meg got home from school. "OK you two," she said, "remember that sleazy hotel I told you about?" Then she saw my face, and could tell that I'd been crying. "Hey, is everything all right?"

I hopped off Nick's lap. "Everything's fine," I said. "Just some adult stuff."

"Remind me never to become an adult," she said.

Nick stood up and put his arms around both of us. "I'll bet my two beautiful ladies are hungry," he said. "Me, I could go for some pizza and salad, made by somebody else and delivered to our door."

"Sounds like a perfect plan to me," I said.

Before Meg could register her vote, the phone rang. The caller ID said that it was Mr. Smith's office, so I answered it.

"Hello Mrs. Rhodes. This is Walter Smith, returning your call." He was as formal as always.

"Hi Mr. Smith," I said. "Thanks for calling back so soon."

"Of course. How can I be of service?"

"Actually Mr. Smith, I would prefer to discuss the matter in person. How soon can my husband and I meet with you in your office?"

"I could meet with you at eight o'clock Monday morning."

"Eight a.m. on Monday?" I looked at Nick and he nodded. "Yes, that will be fine."

As I hung up the phone, Nick was already entering the appointment into the calendar on his work phone.

"So, are you going to tell me what all this is about?" asked Meg.

I grabbed the papers off the table and shoved them back into the envelope. "Nothing that concerns you," I said. "Now, will it be pepperoni, mushroom, or plain?"

"You girls decide on the tough issues," said Nick, grabbing a beer from the refrigerator and twisting off the cap. "I'm going to wet the whistle."

Meg rolled her eyes. "Seriously Dad? 'Wet the whistle?' Who says that? Are you actually trying to give me a traumatized childhood?"

"All right, pepperoni and mushroom it is," I said.

Nick and Meg were in bed and asleep, the leftover pizza was put away in the refrigerator, and I was alone in the kitchen with my fresh cup of Sleepy Time tea. The only light in the room came from the dim bulb in the vent hood over the range, and I was vaguely aware of three chimes from the Regulator clock in the living room. Was it really 3 a.m.?

Now Nick had all the facts, and he was still willing to stand by me. There were no more questions left to answer. I could start moving on with my life, start healing. But what exactly would that mean?

I looked around the kitchen, at the empty chairs. I almost wanted to see you, sitting there in your white dress, staring silently at me. But I was alone with my thoughts.

I took another sip of my tea.

Fateful Storm

Tipped grey metal watering can
Filled with alcohol droplets to quench
Transgressions' overwhelming thirst
Seeding, yet again, jaded blades
For a luscious green manicured lawn
As a red cracked taillight blinks
Exposing a false white truth at dawn

Chapter V

In his office on Monday morning, Mr. Smith introduced us to his nephew, Parker Grayson, who was also a lawyer and looked like one. He was thin, not too tall, and around our age, with a full head of sandy blond hair. He was immaculately dressed in a suit and tie, with polished dress shoes and perfectly manicured hands.

He shook my hand and said, "Please, call me Parker."

"Jean," I said. "And this is my husband, Nick."

"And after all these years," said Mr. Smith, "I'd be happier if you would call me Walter." He motioned us to sit on a striped gold, green, and orange couch, while he and Parker sat on matching gold chairs facing us. "Parker will be taking over my practice once I retire, so I trust you will be comfortable including him in this meeting?"

Nick and I both nodded our agreement.

"Very well. Mrs. Rhodes, you said on the phone that you wanted to discuss evidence concerning Mrs. Marksman's death. Is that correct?" Walter inquired.

"Yes," I replied.

"Is this evidence already collected, or new evidence?" Walter asked.

"It's new evidence. It just surfaced yesterday, although I knew of its existence years ago. I'd like to share the details with you, starting at the beginning."

All three men sat back, expressionless, while I told them the story of that night, from the moment I found your mother lifeless in her bed until I ran into your room. "Mrs. Marksman had prepared boxes labeled for relatives," I said. "I made sure there were no more letters, then I stacked the boxes neatly in the closet and ran back into the bedroom and called 911. I never showed the authorities the letter."

"Did you forget to hand the authorities the letter in the commotion, then were afraid to hand it in later?" asked Walter.

"No, I didn't forget. I took the letter, thinking that I was protecting Hope and her mother. I believed that it was no one's business to read the letter, especially if it concerned her husband's infidelities."

"That doesn't really sound like the thought process of a twelve-year-old girl. Are you sure it wasn't a decision made later?" asked Parker.

"Please, don't take this the wrong way, but I'm aware of exactly what I was thinking that night. I'd gone through too much over the past year to think like a normal twelve-year-old," I said.

"You're looking back now," said Nick, "and you believe that you know what your thinking was back then. Honey, maybe it wasn't all as well thought-out as you're remembering. Time can distort memories."

"Time hasn't distorted anything," I said.

"Mrs. Rhodes," asked Parker, "you said that you didn't hand the letter over to the authorities. So where has it been all these years?"

"In Cassie Bellows' lockbox," I said. "It's what she left for me in her will. Walter, you gave it to me in that manila envelope." I went on to recount the whole story about my trek to Dead Man's Peak, my attempt to burn the letter, and my encounter with Mrs. Bellows.

"So, the letter remained in the pit and you returned home?" asked Walter.

"Yes, when I went back to the pit the next day, the letter and any evidence of the fire were gone. I always assumed that Mrs. Bellows went back."

"Just to clarify," said Parker, "you held this letter at age twelve for three nights, and then it was gone until just the other day?"

"Correct. I now know for certain that Mrs. Bellows took it. It was still unsealed then when I took it out of the manila envelope, so it is safe to assume that she never read it."

"When Mrs. Bellows interrupted you that night, did she know what it was that you were trying to burn?" asked Walter.

"I believe so. She glanced at the handwriting on the envelope and told me to 'Let sleeping dogs lie.'"

"So, the evidence suggests that Cassie Bellows went back, either that night or early the next day, cleared the scene, took the letter with her, and kept it in her lockbox, without reading it, until her death," said Walter. "And then she gave the unopened letter to you out of her estate."

"Yes, I guess that sums it up." I said. "Look, I can only guess why she would have done all that. Maybe she was trying to protect Mrs. Marksman from scandal. Maybe it had to do with her religious beliefs about suicide. Maybe she was afraid her name was somehow involved."

Walter nodded. "You're right, we will never know what she was thinking."

"I think it's best that you and Parker read the letter, too. Then I can ask for your advice and have you deal with any legal issues in handing it over to the authorities." With shaking hands, I pulled the letter out of my purse and handed it to Walter. "I need to move on from all this."

Walter put the letter, still folded, down on the desk next to him. "Mrs. Rhodes, before we read it, please sign this form naming us as your legal counsel. It's just formality, but it ensures confidentiality and enables us to work on your behalf."

"Of course," I replied. While I signed and dated the form, I said, "I'm not sure how her death was ruled, or if this letter will change anything, but I'm praying that I won't be charged with tampering with evidence. When you're through reading it, I ask you to be honest about what kind of charges I might be facing."

"Certainly. Try to relax while we look it over," said Walter.

Thank goodness Nick was sitting there holding my hand for support while I fought back tears and we watched Walter read the letter. Once he had finished, he handed it over to Parker without saying a word. When Parker finished, he handed the letter back to his uncle.

Walter put the letter back on his desk and said, "Mrs. Rhodes, we'll make sure that this evidence is provided to the authorities, and we will speak on your behalf. I can tell you that I don't see anything in here that would suggest any sort of legal liability in this for the actions of a twelve-year-old child. Do you agree, Parker?"

Parker nodded. "I do agree. And even if there were an issue we're not seeing at first glance, there is a statute of limitations that should protect you."

"Quite true," said Walter. "As to the estate left you by Damian Marksman, this letter is not legally binding, and so should have no effect on the will of Damian Marksman. The estate left to you, all of it, still legally belongs to you."

"What are the next steps?" I asked.

Walter stood up. "First, I'd like you to compose a written statement detailing what you just told us about the night of Mrs. Marksman's death, and all the rest. Then, the three of us will sign it as witnesses. Parker and I will take this statement, along with Mrs. Marksman's letter, to the authorities. I'm fairly certain that you won't have to meet directly with them."

As I sat at Walter's desk working on my "confession," the three men quietly chatted about the town, about the weather, and about Mr. Smith's retirement plans. When I was done, I handed the letter to Nick. When Nick was finished reading it, he handed it to Walter, who read it quickly and passed it along to Parker.

Once the document was signed and witnessed, I stood up and shook the two lawyers' hands. "Thank you, Walter. Thank you, Parker. I feel much better now. I'll feel even better when this is finally over."

"And we thank you for entrusting this matter to us," said Walter.

"Before we go," I said, "I need your help with something else. I want to find a reputable private investigator to locate Grace, so I can try to make amends of sorts. We plan to give her the college money Damian left to me, and let her know her biological mother loved her. After she's been found, I'd like your firm to act on my behalf."

"You do realize you're trying to give college money to a woman who's now in her mid-forties?" said Parker.

"Yes, but now she can use the money her mother wanted her to have for anything she needs or wants," I replied.

"I also want to point out that Damian Marksman might not have honored his wife's wishes. He may still have left everything to you," said Parker.

"Actually, my husband made that very point yesterday. But I guess we'll never know the truth about that, will we?" I said.

Parker looked at his phone, then jotted something on a piece of paper. "Here's the name of a private investigator I know who excels in cases like this. If Grace Marksman can be found, Mr. Bloom will find her."

I reached over and took the small paper from him. "Thank you," I said.

A few days after the initial meeting, Nick and I found ourselves sitting on the same striped couch in Walter Smith's office. This time, however, Parker Grayson was not present.

Walter stayed on his feet. "I want to start this meeting by putting your worries completely to rest. The police aren't pursuing any charges against you for tampering with evidence. They have simply added the letter to the existing file regarding Mrs. Marksman's death and autopsy." He smiled down at me. "You were only a child, my dear. Nobody suspects that you in any way acted in malice."

I heaved a deep sigh of relief. "Oh thank goodness," I replied.

"I second that," said Nick.

"Furthermore," said Walter, "we have been informed that the letter does not in any way affect the cause of death listed on Gloria Marksman's death certificate, or implicate anyone else as a possible participant in her death."

"Thank you so much. This really is great news," I said.

"I hope you can finally find some closure and move on," said Walter.

"You said it does not affect the initial cause of death ruling. Can I ask if there's a way for me to find out what that ruling was, even though I'm not a relative?" I asked.

"Yes, with proper identification and for a small fee, anyone can request a copy of the death certificate at the town clerk's office," he said.

"Thank you, again, Walter. The adult in me prays that the ruling was suicide. It's been haunting me for years," I said.

The next day I went to the Graytown clerk's office and filed a request for a copy of Gloria Marksman's death certificate.

For the next few weeks I watched the mailbox, racing out to collect the mail every day, then anxiously sorting through it to see if the answer had arrived. Finally it was there, folded in with a Kroger circular, an official-looking letter with the return address of the town clerk's office.

I sprinted into the house with all the mail in hand. Just inside the den, I tossed the rest of the mail onto Nick's La-Z-Boy chair, and ripped open the envelope I'd been waiting for. With unsteady hands, I unfolded the form and scanned down the page.

There it was, right below Date of Death:

Cause of Death: Suicide.

My legs buckled under me, and I knelt down on the den rug sobbing. Through tears I repeated, "Thank you, God. Thank you, God. I'll do my best to make what I can right with Grace. Thank you, God."

I stared at the blank Word document on the computer screen. If only the right words would come, maybe I could manage to escape this world and create the life I wanted for Grace. I closed my eyes and leaned back in my chair.

The phone rang and I jumped to answer it. It was Mr. Bloom, the private investigator we'd hired on the recommendation of Parker Grayson. Nick and I had already met with him once, two days after the initial meeting with Walter and Parker. We had hired him on the spot to locate Grace.

I almost dropped the receiver, "H-hello?" I stammered into the phone.

"Good afternoon. Is Mrs. Rhodes available, please? This is Mr. Bloom."

"Hi, Mr. Bloom, this is Jean Rhodes. I hadn't expected to hear from you quite so soon. Can I assume that you have some news for us?"

"Yes, I do. But I prefer to discuss this information in person with you and your husband."

A few hours later, Nick and I were sitting in Mr. Bloom's office. He was a robust man with a neatly-trimmed beard, wearing a light blue shirt and a blood-red necktie. His sport jacket was hung on a hook by the door.

"I hope you have wonderful news to report, Mr. Bloom," I said with a faint smile.

I could tell from the look on Mr. Bloom's face this news wasn't going to be as wonderful as I'd hoped. "Mr. and Mrs. Rhodes, there's no easy way to say any of this, so I'm going to just tell you everything I've uncovered."

"That's what we're looking for," Nick said.

"It turns out that finding Grace was the easy part. I worked with the adoption agency identified in the letter. Mrs. Marksman had provided her social security number during the adoption process, which wasn't always the case back then. She also provided her address and means of contact throughout the years."

"Well, that's great news so far," said Nick.

Mr. Bloom nodded and went on. "Yes, well, as we expected, the adoption agency could not provide the contact information to me directly. They agreed to contact Grace about her late biological mother's estate, and Grace would then have the option of reaching out to me to learn more."

"So, are we waiting then to hear from Grace? Or did she say that she wanted no more contact with us?" I asked.

"No, Mrs. Rhodes. It was the adoption agency who called me back, and not Grace. They provided me with the name of a lawyer in New York who is acting on Grace's behalf."

"Okay, I'm confused" I said. "Please tell me that Grace is still alive."

"Yes, she's alive."

"Thank goodness," I said.

"The lawyer asked for my purpose in locating Grace. When I told him the general details of our situation, he told me that he'd get back to me. A few days later he called back and said that he'd spoken to Grace's guardian. He told me he could discuss the case with me via a confidential consent form. When I reviewed the wording on the consent form, I asked to have it revised to include both of you."

"Guardian and a consent form? I'm not following. Was Grace born with some sort of disability?" I asked.

"No, she wasn't, Mrs. Rhodes," Mr. Bloom said, as he pushed a piece of paper across the desk.

"Do we need to sign this consent form?" I asked.

"No, this is a copy for your records. The language now includes you both." Mr. Bloom leaned back in his chair. "Then they asked me to meet the lawyer in person, in New York, to discuss the matter. Grace's guardian wasn't present."

"So, at this meeting, were you provided with more information on Grace's condition?" I asked.

"Yes, I was briefed on her situation. After I returned to the office, I also followed up with some research of my own."

"Is there any way you can cut to the chase?" said Nick.

"Mr. Bloom, we appreciate all your hard work, but we really are anxious to hear the facts," I said.

"Of course. It turns out that Grace's adoptive father was killed in a work-related accident when Grace was ten. Her adoptive mother remarried three years later, to a man who lost his job a year after that. From what I can piece together, it appears that he had a problem with alcohol. His police record shows that he spent some time in jail for public intoxication, for a physical altercation in a bar near his home, and an arrest for driving under the influence of intoxicants."

"Not my idea of a nurturing father," said Nick.

"That's an understatement. One week before Grace's nineteenth birthday, her stepfather beat her almost to death. She suffered severe brain damage in the attack, and was in a coma for more than eight months. She now functions at the level of a nine-year-old, and lives in an assisted living facility. Her stepsister is her guardian."

"What a bastard," said Nick.

"It might help to know that the stepfather was convicted of aggravated battery and attempted murder. He's still in prison, serving a thirty-year sentence," said Mr. Bloom.

The room began to spin and I gasped for breath. The color drained from my face. "Honey, do you need a glass of water?" asked Nick.

"No, what I need is to turn back time and make all of this as it should've been," I sobbed.

"Mrs. Rhodes, you are not to blame for any of this."

"He's right, Jean," said Nick, putting his arm around me.

"I deserve to be locked up," I said. "That poor girl!"

"Jean, just stop it! There is no way anything you did or didn't do caused this to happen. Grace was adopted by these people before you were even born, and what happened to her would probably not have been any different even if Damian had given her everything."

"How do you know that? How can anybody know?"

Nick let me cry into his shoulder for a few minutes, while the two men waited in awkward silence. Finally, Nick asked, "Does Grace's guardian know about the money we intend to give her?"

"Yes, she does," said Mr. Bloom. "Her lawyer and I discussed it, and made it clear that all the details will be worked out through Mr. Smith's office."

"Mr. Bloom, thank you for all of your hard work," I said.

"It's my job, Mrs. Rhodes," Mr. Bloom said. "Just for the record, I think it's an honorable thing you folks are doing. I'm sure the money can at least help out with Grace's care."

"I hope so," I said.

"You know it will," said Nick. "But this is also about helping you heal, Jean. Promise me that you'll leave your guilt behind when we leave this office."

I changed the subject. "Can you tell us what Grace's name is now?" I asked.

"Her adoptive parents named her Elle. Elle Sauder. In fact I have a picture here that was taken shortly before she was injured."

He pulled a five-by-seven photo from the file on his desk and handed it to me. The resemblance to Hope was astounding! Those piercing deep blue eyes told me that there could be no doubt that she and Hope had the same father.

And the same father as Michael Grainger.

My stomach made a somersault as it occurred to me that Michael should be informed of his other half-sister. Elle certainly wouldn't be capable of making that decision, or of initiating contact with him. Didn't I owe that much to Hope, to bring her siblings together?

I knew that Nick wouldn't support this line of thinking, so I decided not to discuss it with him. His attitude would be that the less Michael was involved in Elle's life the better off she would be, and that made a certain amount of sense.

Then I thought of something Bruce Coville once said; *"Withholding information is the essence of tyranny. Control of the flow of information is the tool of the dictatorship."* Did I have the right to be a tyrant?

I was surprised to see Michael Grainger's number and address listed in the phone book. He lived in Graytown, in a subdivision called Nottaway. Somehow, I'd pictured him living as a recluse somewhere far away, not in a neighborhood right here in town. But then, as my grandmother once told me, "Evil doesn't always choose to hide outside of plain sight. It often lives right under our noses."

I dialed the number. After the phone rang eight times, I was almost startled to hear a woman's voice say, "Hello?"

"Yes, may I please speak to Michael Grainger?" I said.

"He's not available right now, but if you're calling about an overdue bill, we just sent out all the checks. My grandmother just died, so the payments were delayed," she said.

"I'm sorry for your loss, but this isn't that sort of call. When would be a better time to call back, please?"

"A better time?" Her voice took on a hard edge. "When hell freezes over would probably work. How about if I just take a message?"

"Can you please tell him Jean Cartwright Rhodes called, and it's important that I speak with him?"

There was a long pause, and then she said, "Hold on." Apparently Michael had told his wife who I was.

When Michael picked up the receiver, the slur in his voice made it clear that he'd been drinking. "Well, I guess hell did freeze over if you're calling me, Jean."

"Yes, Michael, I guess you're right. Look, I need to speak with you in person. I'm willing to drive to you if you'll promise to be sober when I get there," I said.

He laughed that cruel laugh. "I would not want anything dulling the pleasure of seeing you again, Jean. OK, deal, no booze. So, to what do I owe the pleasure? You been throwing rocks around in that glass house of yours?"

"You'll know when I get there. How about I drive to your place this Saturday afternoon around two?" I said.

"Looking forward to it. Why don't you wear a white 'I'm holier than thou' dress for the occasion?" he commanded.

I ignored his comment. "And make sure your wife's there."

On Saturday afternoon, I programmed Michael's address into the GPS in my Traverse. Nottaway was on the south side of Graytown, a ten-minute drive from my house. I wondered how long he'd been living there. I was grateful I had somehow managed to avoid crossing paths with him over the past fifteen years.

I tried to enjoy the colors of the fall foliage as I drove, listening to the occasional instructions from the GPS. I had never actually been in Nottaway, so I was relying on the guidance of that calm, emotionless voice to find my way.

I was beginning to wonder if the GPS might be confused when it told me to turn left onto an almost invisible dirt road. As I turned, I made a mental note of the tiny granite-walled store on the corner.

Not far down the dirt road I had to make another left, this time into a narrow, unpaved lane. I was amazed at how close I had to cut the wheel, and I couldn't help but wonder how anyone without an SUV could ever make this trip. The lane was well-worn, with deep ruts and islands of sand and grass that would surely scrape the underside of a small car.

There was no house in sight, and I was beginning to look for a place to turn around, when I came around a curve and a small, deteriorating log cabin appeared almost out of nowhere.

An old blue Ford pickup truck sat next to the cabin, and I could see smoke billowing from the old brick chimney. I parked the Traverse behind the blue truck and walked toward the front door.

The door had a nice warm "welcome" sign pinned to it, just below an old tarnished doorknocker. There was no doorbell, so I took a deep breath for courage and used the doorknocker.

Michael's wife answered the door, smiling politely. "Hello. You must be Jean. Please, come in," she said.

"Thank you," I said.

The house had an open floor plan, and from the entranceway I could see Michael sitting back in a well-worn recliner. "Jean, I'd like you to meet my wife, Sadie."

I assumed Sadie's same polite smile and took her hand. "Nice to meet you, Sadie," I said.

Michael crossed his feet and put his hands behind his head. "Sorry I'm not in any mood for small talk. It's almost the end of the day, and to honor your request, I haven't had anything to drink yet."

Sadie led me into the room and cleared a pile of newspapers from the couch. "Please, sit down," she said. "Can I offer you a soda, or coffee?"

"Thank you. I'd love a soda if it's not any trouble. Diet if you have it."

"No trouble at all," she said, and left the room.

Michael sat up restlessly in his chair and massaged his index finger with the thumb of his other hand.

"Michael," I said, "if you need a drink to keep you from imploding, go ahead and have one."

"Judging from the look on your face, I think you might want my wife to put a little something in yours, too," Michael said. He turned his head toward the kitchen and called, "Honey, did you hear that? Bring me a glass, along with the bottle of Jack."

Sadie returned balancing three glasses of soda on a tray. She had a bottle of Jack under her arm. She handed her husband his glass, which was only half filled with soda.

Michael filled his glass with whiskey, then handed the bottle to his wife, who put it on the floor next to the couch and sat down.

"Okay, so now that you have our attention, please enlighten us," said Michael. "What's this all about?"

"Okay, but I want you to know that I'm not going to sugar-coat anything. This is all about getting to the truth."

"The truth, the whole truth, and nothing but the truth. That's why I got whisked off to that sanitarium." He took a sip of his drink, made a "gun" pointed in the air with his free hand, and laughed. "Go ahead, shoot. Pop. Pop."

"Just so we're clear, Michael, you don't intimidate me."

"Oh, but I think I do, Jean. I definitely do," Michael said. "Here, let me help you get started. I'll bet you found out I was Hope's half-brother, and feel like you need to share that revelation with me. And, of course, you want to tell me that I should be filled with regret. Blah. Blah. Blah. Am I on the right track?"

I sat back on the couch. "Well, I thought you probably knew by now, and I was going to give you the benefit of the doubt when it came to regret. But I can see now that regret is just not part of you, and probably never will be."

He gulped down the last of his drink. "You are observant. But if you're looking for me to take on all the guilt, you're wasting your time. If you recall, Hope was dead before I picked up that rock. And yeah, it was my hands over her mouth and nose, but it was a game we were all playing. How quick you are to dismiss your own guilt and walk around like some kind of a saint." He pointed a finger directly at my eyes.

I could almost feel his finger stab straight through me. "I don't think I'll ever forget that day, or forgive myself for it. But remember, I never played that twisted game, ever."

"There's the 'holier than the rest of us' Jean that I remember," he said.

"Look, I will always regret I didn't take my turn in place of Hope," I said. "But you should have been charged with manslaughter. Not only did you smother her, but you picked up that rock and smashed her forehead after she was lying on the ground."

"Lying on the ground?" he shouted. "She was dead. Let me spell it out for you, Jean. D-E-A-D."

"What if she could have been resuscitated? Didn't that ever occur to you?"

"Resuscitated? You're out of your mind. Even the autopsy said she was dead before I hit her."

"Well, you didn't have an autopsy report when you picked up that rock. I think the Marksmans were too generous with you."

"Generous? Really? Imagine your own flesh and blood regretting your existence. My own father would have had me stoned to death if he could have. I heard that it was Hope's mom who got him to agree to the final settlement."

"You murdered his daughter, flesh and blood or not. I read Gloria's letter, so I'm not surprised that she stood up for you."

"What letter?" he asked.

I ignored him and went on. "To think that I actually pitied you when I found out that you were Hope's brother. Well, I guess I was wrong to think that knowledge would cause you any pain or remorse."

"So, you actually see me as being a victim? Oh, Jean, I can change how you think about that day. I really, really, really can."

"What, Michael? I was there, remember?" I wasn't going to allow him to rattle me.

He lowered his voice. "I already knew who my biological father was before that day. I knew!" His laughter echoed off the walls.

My heart skipped a beat. There it was. The thought that I had tried to push out of my mind hadn't been irrational after all. Michael had just confirmed that he is, and always was, pure evil.

"Why Jean, you're looking kind of pale. Now what could have caused that?" He sat back in his chair and smiled. "Are you thinking that you wasted your trip out here in your nice new car? A car, by the way, that you only have because my father gave you everything that should have come to me."

I paused to collect my thoughts. Then I remembered that Michael's wife, Sadie, was right next to me. I turned and saw her sitting there, silently trembling, with a stricken look on her face. I couldn't help wondering if she had ever before really seen the monster she had married. I turned back to face Michael. "Well, if it was jealousy that's been fueling you all these years, I just might be able to burst your bubble."

"Well, this should be entertaining," he said.

I ignored his sarcasm. "So we can assume that you spent your childhood envying Hope for everything she had that you didn't – including the acceptance of your father. And now, you're jealous of me for inheriting what you believe belonged to you. I'll bet you're even angry with the people of Graytown for turning their backs when you were sent away and acting like you never existed. How am I doing so far?"

"Now there you go again, trying to make it sound like I'm a victim. I'm not sure how you think this is going to burst any bubbles, but go on," he said.

"Oh, I haven't gotten to that part yet."

"I'm sorry. Please, by all means, continue."

"I've just learned that Hope actually has an older sister, who was given up for adoption before any of us were born. Michael, you have another half-sister."

I could see from the look on Michael's face I had penetrated his armor.

"What the hell are you talking about? How do you know that?"

"When Hope's mother died, she left a letter behind. It explained a lot of things, including the fact that Hope had an older sister. The letter was what Mrs. Bellows left for me."

"What was Cassie doing with it?"

"That's a long story."

"So, did Cassie know that I was Hope's half-brother and that I have another half-sister?" I paused for what I thought was only a moment, but he yelled, "Answer me, goddamit!"

Is that sadness on his face, or just anger? "No, Michael, I'm sure Mrs. Bellows never read the letter. She only knows as much as you told to her."

Michael stretched and grabbed the bottle of Jack from the floor next to Sadie. He took the cap off the bottle, poured his glass half full and took a gulp. His look of confidence returned. "Do you know who this half-sister is? No, don't tell me, she grew up in a huge mansion and is happily married with children. Or wait, she joined the Peace Corps. Won a Nobel prize?"

I took in a deep breath. "Yes, I did find your sister. Her name is Elle Sauder. And no, she didn't have a better life than you've had. Or, in a sense, any better than Hope had."

"So tell me all about her. Isn't that why you came here?"

I paused to gather my thoughts. "Actually, she was beaten nearly to death by her stepfather just before her nineteenth birthday. She sustained severe brain damage, so she functions at the level of a nine-year-old."

I was surprised that I didn't feel the slightest satisfaction at seeing the stricken look on his face. The sharp anger in his eyes faded, replaced by a look of pain. On any other person, I would say that it was a look of genuine sadness, even regret.

But this was Michael. I pressed on. "The day Hope's mother died was Elle's sixteenth birthday. Nobody read the letter Mrs. Marksman wrote that day, because I took it and tried to destroy it. Cassie Bellows interrupted me, and for reasons we may never understand, gave it back to me last week in her will, still unopened."

"Wow, and I'm the monster? Why the hell would you do something like that?" Michael said.

"At the time I thought I was protecting everyone. Now I have to find a way to live with that decision. You see, besides explaining about giving Elle up for adoption, the letter also asked that Damian Marksman leave all their possessions, including Hope's college fund, to her."

"But Damian gave you everything years after Elle was injured. What exactly are you leaving out?"

"If she'd received that college fund, maybe she would have been away at school that night her stepfather beat her. Maybe she would be living in a mansion with children. Her life would have been different." I was starting to lose my composure.

Michael snorted. "And you believe Damian Marksman would have jumped to honor his wife's last wish? Remember who we're talking about here."

"He might have. It was tainted money. He said some things on his deathbed, that you were conceived after a fight about that college fund when Gloria was pregnant with Hope. He never wanted to set it up."

Michael shook his head. "I'm not so sure," he said.

"Don't worry, we've dissolved the account and have arranged to give the money to your half-sister's caregiver," I stated.

Michael remained silent. I opened my purse and took out the photograph Mr. Bloom had given me. "Michael, here's a picture of your sister, Elle, taken before she was beaten."

Michael reached over and took the photograph out of my hand and stared at it. Then, completely out of character, he began to sob, hiding his face with his hands. Sadie sat next to me, still silent, with tears running down her cheeks. I was on the verge of crying myself.

Part of me wanted to celebrate, because I had triggered honest emotion in Michael that I had never believed existed. That fleeting feeling was almost immediately buried in an avalanche of guilt. I was the one person truly to blame for everything that guided Michael's life from the moment Hope let go of that colored leaf from her hand and leaned back against the wrinkled bark of the oak tree.

After a few minutes, Michael composed himself and said, "So, the bastard discarded her, too, even at the very end. He knew about her, and he still gave everything to you."

I stood up and picked up my jacket and purse. "Look, I'm not going to try to defend Damian Marksman. I have no way of knowing what he would have done. I just know what I have to do." Michael just stared at me over the rim of his glass. "Look Michael, if you decide you'd like to contact your half-sister, have your lawyer speak to my lawyer, Walter Smith. He's already contacted your sister's caregiver, and your lawyer can do the same for you."

I tossed Walter Smith's business card on the coffee table.

"Jean, why didn't you just have your lawyer contact me directly? Why did you come here?" Michael asked.

I wanted to tell Michael that I was sorry, but the words wouldn't come, so I just turned away and shut the door behind me. I could hear the welcome sign swaying from side to side as I walked back to my car.

As the ignition fired up, so did the sky above. The thunder and lightning split the sky, then the clouds opened and poured rain hard on the earth below. I considered getting out of the car and letting the lightning strike me down for all the pain I had caused since the day you died.

Instead, I put the car in drive and wound my way back down that muddy lane. With the rain drumming on the hood of the car, Brad Paisley's "Whiskey Lullaby" started playing on the radio, and I was struck with the idea that Michael Grainger was back in that cabin, trying to drink his own pain away, while his wife could only watch. The heavens were crying, but not just for my regrets, or even for Michael's. They were tears for a little girl lost to her parents, another little girl lost to the world, and all the things unsaid and undone that could have changed all that.

Back in my own kitchen, I searched to find something, anything, to distract me from my thoughts. I sat at the kitchen table, absently tearing small pieces of Scotch tape off the roll, then carefully placing them along the edge of the table in a row.

The roll was almost empty when Nick's voice brought me back to reality. "What on earth are you doing?" he asked.

"I'm thinking of wrapping a few Christmas gifts early to keep me busy," I said. "Maybe if I can Scotch tape the presents closed, and if the tape holds for the next few months, then I can wrap my entire body up and see if I can hold my sanity inside."

"What are you talking about?"

"I went to see him, Nick," I said.

"Who did you go see?"

"Michael," I said.

Nick took a step back. "You did what?"

"I'm sorry. I should have told you, but it was something I just had to do. The second I saw Elle's picture, I knew that he was her half-brother. He needed to know about her."

"Did you go alone?"

"Yes, I did. But his wife was there, too."

"That's as good as being alone with him. He's a killer for God's sake!"

"I really don't think I was ever in any real danger."

"Seriously, Jean? You could have had our lawyer tell him. You could have sent me. Anything could have happened to you. And nobody knew where you were going! We would not even know where to start searching for you. What on earth were you thinking?"

"Nick, I'm sorry. I just felt like I had to take away the power he had over me."

Nick went to the sink and poured himself a glass of water. "Jean, when you were keeping secrets from me about your childhood, I understood. But this is now, and you're keeping things from me."

"You would have stopped me from going, and I had to."

"You're damned right I would have! But that's not even the point here. When we start lying to each other, keeping things from each other, it's over. How can a marriage survive once trust is lost?"

"You're right, Nick. I promise I'll never keep anything like this from you again."

Nick had a look in his eye that I'd never seen before. "I'm heading upstairs," he said.

"Nick, please say we're going to be okay," I called out after him. His response was to slam the bedroom door.

I sat staring at the kitchen table for a few minutes, then picked up what was left of the roll of tape and went back to work tearing and arranging the strips along the edge of the table. I heard the shower go on upstairs, and when I involuntarily looked up, I cut my thumb on the tape dispenser.

I looked, fascinated, as a drop of blood formed on my thumb, then dropped to the table. The same table where I'd sat and listened to Mrs. Marksman talking about *Macbeth* all those years ago. Some stains couldn't be washed out.

I got up and grabbed a paper towel from the sink and wiped the blood from the table, but when I looked at the paper towel it was stained with more blood from my thumb. I tried to rinse the blood out of the paper towel, but it just shredded into a pink mess in the sink.

I looked through the kitchen window above the sink at the old oak tree, and said, "Out, damned spot."

Graze Castle

Long, long ago, or once upon a time
A group of children committed a crime
Never changing eyes it constantly sees
That mocking, haunting old oak tree
Through boxed paned glasses it looks
Watched by the figure whose life they took
Against the haunting memorial leaning in
While inside, a metal locked box hides a sin
Overcast grey clouds in the sky dip behind
Along with a protective fence tree lined
Concealing a house of grandeur size
Muffling the voices of so many lies

Chapter VI

When my cell phone rang, I didn't recognize the number that showed up on the caller ID. Out of curiosity, I decided to answer before it went to voice mail.

"Hello, this is Jean Rhodes."

There was a delay before I heard a familiar voice on the other end of the receiver.

"Jean, this is Sadie Grainger."

I paused and took a deep breath before I replied, "Hello, Sadie." It had been almost three months since my visit to Sadie and Michael's house, and I'd finally stopped agonizing over the events of that night.

"I'm calling to tell you that Michael's at St. Mary's Hospital."

"I don't mean to be rude, Sadie, but why are you calling me about that?"

"He shot himself."

I nearly dropped the phone. I hoped that Sadie didn't hear my gasp. "How? What happened?"

"After you told him about Elle, Michael tracked down Elle's stepfather, Carl. He visited Carl in prison, found out that he was to be released today, and where he was going to stay. Michael waited for him at a bus stop, where he shot and killed him. Then Michael turned the gun on himself." Her voice was completely emotionless.

"Sadie, I'm not sure what you want from me."

There was a short pause. "He's in intensive care, in a medically induced coma. There's a police officer guarding his room. I worked it out so you can visit him." There was a hint of sadness in her voice.

"Visit him!" I said.

"Other than my mother-in-law and me, no one else will visit him. I just asked myself, why the hell not invite Jean Cartwright Rhodes? You can see for yourself how your plans have worked out, and say anything you need to say to him while he's still breathing."

"I'm confused. Is he at St. Mary's hospital in New York, or in Massachusetts? Carl was incarcerated in New York."

"It happened in Massachusetts, about an hour from here. Apparently Carl was heading to stay at an uncle's place."

"Sadie, I'm still not exactly sure why you called me. You know how I feel about Michael."

"I'm not doing it for you. I'm doing it for my husband. You claim to be a Christian and all. I thought if you told him everything you needed to say, it might make things better."

"Sadie, I'm not God passing judgment on Michael. Yes, I'm a Christian, but I'm not free from sin. I think Michael needs more than me there at the end."

She ignored my words. "You need to know that it was love, not hate, that forced Michael to kill Carl. Not that I expect you to believe that."

"Sadie, I don't mean to sound harsh, but the Michael I know has always been motivated by anger, not love. For your sake, I'm truly sorry you ever got involved with him."

"Just so we're clear, the fact that I'm talking to you now doesn't mean that we're friends. I won't lose any sleep waiting for you to decide what you want to do."

With a curious sense of detachment I heard myself say, "I'll be there as soon as I can."

Sadie's reply was to simply hang up. I sat with the phone in my hand, replaying the conversation in my mind. I felt like I'd been punched in the stomach. Michael had killed again! And this time it was intentional, obviously carefully planned. And Sadie thought it was my fault, that I had set the stage for the murder by telling Michael about his other half-sister.

Could she be right?

I called Nick.

"Hey, honey," he said. "What's up?"

"Oh Nick, I'm sorry to drop this bomb on you while you're working. I just got a phone call from Michael's wife, Sadie."

There was a brief pause. "Why on earth would she call you?" Nick asked.

"Nick, Michael's in a coma. He shot and killed Elle's stepfather, Carl, when he was released from prison today. Then he shot himself."

Nick paused again. "That's a lot to process. Did she threaten you?"

"No, actually it was the opposite. She arranged for me to see Michael."

"She did what? You can't be serious."

"I am serious."

"Please tell me you told her to go to hell."

"No, I didn't. I told her I'd be right over."

"Are you out of your mind?"

"Nick, I need to do this. Maybe this time I can find some closure. Look, I know you're not happy about the idea."

"That's an understatement!"

"I know, and I'm sorry."

Nick sighed. "Well, at least you're being honest with me. Look, do you have to go today? Why don't you sleep on it?"

"The opportunity may pass if I don't go today. As awful as this may sound, I pray that he dies right after I see him."

"Not awful at all. We would be better off if he had died from the bullet and never made it to the hospital. So you really feel like you have to confront this devil?"

"He can't hurt me. He's in a coma."

"Somehow, I don't find that completely reassuring." Nick paused, then sighed once more into the phone. "Fine, do what you have to do. Just be careful, and call me when you get home."

"It's a hospital, Nick, I'll be fine. I promise to call you as soon as I'm home."

"So what are you going to say to a comatose demon?"

I thought for a few seconds. "I have no idea."

I hung up the phone and gazed through the kitchen window at the oak tree.

"It's a magic eight ball, Jean." Eleven-year-old Hope giggled and waved it in the air. "You can find the answer to anything by asking it a question. Watch!" She held the eight ball close to her mouth and said, "Magic eight ball, will Jean get married someday? Now, you shake it hard, three times. One, two, three… See! The answer is 'Yes!'"

The laughter of two little girls echoed through the branches. "I'm sure it says that all the time," I said, gasping for breath.

"Okay then, let's ask it another question. Magic eight ball, will Jean marry… ME?" She shook the eight ball again. "The answer is 'Better Not Tell You Now.'" Helpless with laughter, we collapsed to the ground, our backs against the tree.

As the memory faded away, I mused that the magic eight ball must have known that Hope didn't have much longer to live.

My head was starting to throb, so I dumped two Tylenol out of the bottle, chopped them up with a steak knife, and washed them down with a glass of water – as always, struggling for breath in the process.

When I arrived at the hospital, Sadie was there to meet me. "Hello, Sadie," I said.

"Jean, it'll be a few minutes before you can go in. The doctor's in there now."

"Sadie, I know it's not my place, but you must know by now that you married a monster."

"I know you see the man who killed two people. But there is a good side to my husband."

"Really? Because the way I see it, those two exceptions pretty much trump any good he might have done. But God forgives us if we confess to Him our sins and believe in Him."

"Yes, so my grandmother always told me," she said.

"Well, I'm not God, and I'm not sure that I can ever forgive Michael."

"I don't care what you think of my husband, but somehow, I feel like you need to hear about a side of him you've never seen."

"Look, it really doesn't matter what I think of Michael. What matters is what God and Michael think of Michael. But considering the pain I've caused you, I'll hear you out."

Sadie stared at the floor for a few seconds, then said, "After Michael learned about Elle, he couldn't get her off his mind. It really meant something to him to find out that he had a sister. And it really upset him that Carl beat Elle so badly." She paused and looked me in the eyes. "Jean, he suspected that there might have been more to it than just the beating."

I shook my head. "Somehow I just can't see Michael as a hero. Besides, whatever Carl did to Elle, he paid for it with a lot of years in prison. Michael never served so much as a day for what he did to Hope. Then, after Carl did his time, Michael took the law into his own hands and executed him. That's not a hero; it's a vigilante."

"I'm not sure why you don't seem to understand that Michael served out his time in that children's facility."

"Well, he should have been tried as an adult."

"So, who's the vigilante now? You either trust the system or you don't."

"Not trusting the system is very different from becoming a self-appointed judge, jury, and executioner."

Sadie's lips tightened and she leaned forward in her chair. "Well, whether or not you believe it, I know in my own heart that it was love for his sister Elle that drove Michael to kill Carl."

I shook my head. "I'm sure the idea of Carl beating and maybe even molesting Elle might have angered Michael into killing him, but how do you call that 'love?' Sadie, please don't take this the wrong way, but I'm not sure that Michael is even capable of loving anyone."

Sadie gripped the arms of the chair and hissed, "Jean, I fell in love with Michael because he has always been my knight in shining armor. He caught a man raping my mother. If he had come to her rescue a few minutes earlier, I would never have been born. But he was the one person who was there to stand up for her."

I was stunned. "Oh, Sadie! I don't know what to say."

"Nothing. You don't say anything. That part of the story doesn't concern you."

We sat in silence until the doctor came out of Michael's room. "You can go in now," he said. "But keep it short."

Sadie thanked the doctor and turned to me. "Before I let you see him, I should fill you in on a few things."

"Of course," I said.

"They told me that one reason he's alive is because his blood-alcohol level was so high. They still don't know how extensive his paralysis is, or if he has suffered permanent brain damage. They don't know if he will ever wake up."

"I understand," I said. "Um, they say that someone in a coma can hear everything you say to them."

Sadie ignored my attempt at conversation. "I love my husband," she said, "and the things he's done haven't changed that. But you should understand that I'm not sure I can live my life married to a man who'll be in prison. A man who will be paralyzed or, even worse, brain damaged like his sister." She paused and looked down at the floor. "I can't help but wonder who you think the real monster is now, Michael or me."

I opened my mouth to speak, but she held up a hand to stop me. "Just to be clear," she said, "that's simply a statement. I don't need or desire any kind of answer from you." She turned on her heel and walked into Michael's room.

I said a polite, "hello," to the policeman on guard just outside the door, and I followed Sadie. He couldn't be charged yet with Carl's murder, but the guard was there in case he woke up.

I sat down on a black plastic chair on the side of the hospital bed, and listened to the rhythmic noise from the life support machines that were keeping Michael alive. I stared at his face and tried to think of something to say. Sadie sat behind me in another chair, waiting and listening.

The lack of conversation in this room spoke loudly. I found myself musing that Michael had succeeded in taking Hope's life without trying, but when he tried to end his own life, he was a complete failure. He had tried to shoot himself through the heart, and missed.

The writer in me couldn't help thinking about the Tin Man from the *Wizard of Oz*. Michael was the opposite of the Tin Man – it was as if having a heart caused him too much pain. For a fleeting moment, I wondered if the shooting of Carl really had, as Sadie insisted, been motivated by love.

Watching the steady rise and fall of his chest as the machine forced air in and out of his lungs, it was obvious that all of us were hoping that Michael would never regain consciousness. I had seen it in Sadie's eyes, and heard it in her voice. I felt it in my heart.

The detective assigned to Michael's case walked into the room, carefully balancing two cups of coffee. He crossed directly over to Sadie and handed her one cup. "Mrs. Grainger, I noticed yesterday that you ordered your coffee with crème and sugar, so I brought you one today."

Sadie smiled and took the coffee. "Thank you, Detective Askew, that's kind of you. It seems that there is no change in my husband's condition today."

The detective's attention was totally focused on Sadie, and he never glanced in Michael's direction. He was a charmingly good-looking man, with dark brown hair and deeply penetrating brown eyes. His nose was prominent, and his skin had a deep olive tone. His smile was captivating, and it was clear that the chemistry between the detective and Sadie was traveling in both directions.

Then Detective Askew seemed to realize that I was in the room. He said, "Oh, I'm sorry. If I had known there were other visitors today, I would have brought another coffee. Are you family, ma'am?"

Before I could respond, Sadie said, "No, she's not family. I arranged for her to visit Michael." She smiled sweetly at me and said, "Detective, I'd like you to meet Jean Cartwright Rhodes. She is indirectly responsible for my husband being in this bed."

Once again I was stunned. I couldn't and didn't want to respond to an accusation that held some truth to it. "I'm pleased to meet you, Detective." I stood up and picked up my purse. "I think this is the perfect time for me to be going. Goodbye."

As I turned to leave, Sadie called after me, stopping me in my tracks. "Jean, just one more thing before you go. I really wish you'd taken your turn that day. Things would be very different. Hope would be here, and Michael may even have become someone important. Of course, I'd probably never have met him. But, oh well."

When she finished speaking, I took a deep breath, exhaled slowly, then made my way out of the room.

The hospital hallway seemed to stretch into the distance. I tried to look calm and composed as I headed for the elevators, but by the time I passed the nurses' station, I could feel my hands starting to shake.

In the elevator I looked at the button with "11" on it. If only this were a time machine, that button might take me back to make things right. But it was just an elevator. I pushed the "Lobby" button and tried to calm my breathing as I went down.

When the doors opened in the lobby, I found myself face-to-face with Michael's mother, Marilyn Grainger. She had aged a lot since the last time I saw her, but it was unmistakably her.

She didn't appear to recognize me, which made perfect sense. The last time she saw me, I was a child. I gave her a polite stranger-in-a-doorway nod, then walked past her and out of the hospital.

Sadie had said that she and Michael had been out of contact with Mrs. Grainger, so I was sure her presence would come as a surprise. Hopefully the detective could head off any sort of conflict, even though having him around seemed to have shut off some of Sadie's filters.

In any case, it wasn't my concern how Sadie might handle her mother-in-law, and it certainly wasn't something I should allow myself to worry about. Driving home, I could picture Michael's mother saying something like, "I expected you to end up like this."

Then it dawned on me that I hadn't taken the opportunity to tell Michael exactly how I felt about him. If he really could hear me through his coma, I had not given him a word to hear.

Back at home, I stood at the kitchen table and sorted through the mail. In the middle of the stack was an envelope addressed to

Jean Cartwright Rhodes. My name and street address were typed on the envelope, and there was no return address.

Once I opened the envelope and pulled out the letter, I immediately knew who had sent it. The handwriting was barely legible, large and angry. It had clearly been written by a left-handed individual. The letter said:

JEAN,

I'LL SURELY SEE YOU ON WHATEVER SIDE WE END UP ON. UNTIL WE MEET AGAIN,

MICHAEL

I looked at the postmark date on the envelope. It had been mailed the same day Michael killed Carl.

With trembling hands I dropped the letter on the table. Could it be true? My faith had been tortured and sometimes pushed aside in the decades-long battle for my sanity, but I had never really doubted my connection with God. It seemed obvious that Michael had long ago given up any hope of reaching heaven. Could he be right that I had too?

As I read and re-read Michael's two-sentence note, I could begin to see the truth. Michael wasn't waiting for me to forgive him for Hope's death, or even to admit my role in her death. Instead, Michael blamed me for everything. It was my fault that Hope had died. It was my fault that he was sent away. It was my fault that Elle's life had been destroyed. It was even my fault that Michael had felt compelled to murder Carl.

All this time, I'd had it wrong. Sadie wasn't trying to help Michael and me find any sort of closure; she was waiting for me to ask Michael and her for forgiveness.

This letter even suited Michael's need for vengeance. He knew full well about the remorse I felt every day of my life. He knew that this letter would trigger that pain and haunt me. These two sentences scrawled on a sheet of paper would serve the same purpose the bullets had for Michael and Carl.

When Nick returned home, I was sitting on the couch in the den waiting for him. Even Valium couldn't calm my anxiety. As he set down his jacket and briefcase I said, "Nick, we need to talk."

Nick slid the ottoman over to the couch and sat in front of me. "So how did it go? Did you get the closure you were hoping for?"

"No, not really. He's still in a coma. I just stared at him and never spoke a single word. The truth is, a part of me wanted him to either wake up or go ahead and die while I was there at his bedside."

"Well, you look shaken up. Didn't you expect that seeing Michael would upset you? Please tell me you didn't pity seeing him after all he's done?"

"No, I didn't feel sorry for him. I have to show you something, and I know you're not going to like it." I handed him Michael's note.

"What's this? I thought I finally knew the whole story?"

"You do. This just came today, but I didn't see it until I got home from the hospital. If I had opened it earlier, I probably would never have gone."

Nick took the paper out of my hand and read Michael's note. "Just perfect, Jean. I'm not going to say, 'I told you so.' I'm just relieved that you were able to walk away both times."

"I'm not sure why I came to Michael's defense, but I did. "I still feel that he didn't want to physically hurt me. I just think he finds joy in playing with my emotions."

"Jean, can you really be that naive?"

"Well, the good news is, it's just about over. Don't you think if he wanted to kill me, he would have done it on his way to kill Carl?"

Nick ignored my last comment. "I'm dropping this off to Walter Smith in case he does come out of the coma and there's a trial."

"It's your call. But Sadie told me if he does wake up, he'll be paralyzed. He may even have serious brain damage."

"I guess that's great news. But hopefully he won't wake up."

"That may happen, too."

"Well, now I have a figurative smoking gun to add to the evidence against him," he said, shaking the letter in his hand. "And if he does wake up, we may want to get a restraining order, as silly as that may sound to you."

In the weeks after visiting Michael in the hospital, I was especially anxious for the delivery of the daily newspaper. I skimmed through the obituaries every day, frantically checking for Michael's name to appear.

Michael's shooting had, of course, made the local news, but quickly faded out of the spotlight. I was surprised that nobody dug up any mention of Hope's death and Michael's role in it, but it stood to reason since his childhood records were sealed.

Nearly a month after my visit to the hospital, I received a voice mail from Sadie. "Jean, it's Sadie Grainger. Michael's awake. He's aware that you were here when he was in the coma, and he has asked if you would come back."

The tone of her voice was eerily calm. Without thinking it through, I dialed her cell phone. I was expecting to reach her voice mail, but she answered on the second ring.

"Hi, Sadie. This is Jean Rhodes," I said.

"So, you got my message."

"Yes, I did. So how is he? Does he understand what he's done and where he is?"

"He's suffered no brain damage, but he's paralyzed from the waist down. The doctor's coming down the hallway now. Will you be coming to see him or not?"

"I really wasn't planning on it."

"Why? Are you afraid to see him now that he's awake?"

"No, Sadie, I'm not afraid of Michael."

"Aren't you just a little bit afraid of whatever he may say to you?"

I could hear Michael's childhood voice from that awful day, taunting me in my mind; *Chicken! Chicken!* "I'm not scared," I said.

"Well, I couldn't care less either way, but he wants to see you. I have to go talk to the doctor now, so what's it going to be?"

"Let me call you back with my answer," I said.

"I won't hold my breath waiting."

I hung up with Sadie and called my husband at work.

"Hey, honey, is everything okay?" Nick asked.

"Yes, everything's okay at home. Nick, Sadie left me a voice mail telling me Michael woke up and wanted to see me, and I called her back."

"Let me guess, you told her you'd be right there?" Nick said.

"No, I didn't. I told her I'd call her back with an answer, and then I called you. Can you leave work by any chance and go with me?"

"How about you just call her back and tell her you won't be showing up."

"I know this probably sounds crazy to you, but please try to understand, I really need to do this. Don't worry, he'll be under a police guard. Plus, he's paralyzed."

"Baby, I really think not going to a face-to-face meeting with the devil himself would be the best choice," he said.

"Well, as any writer will tell you, every story needs a beginning, a middle, and an end. I need a proper end to this story."

There was a long pause before Nick said, "Ok, I can work it out to leave in an hour or so. I'll come pick you up."

I sighed deeply. "Thank you for this. I love you."

I called Sadie back and left her a voice mail to let her know that I'd be there in a few hours.

Waiting for Nick, Sadie's taunt repeated over and over in my mind, *"I won't hold my breath..."* I wasn't sure if she'd purposely chosen those words, or if the striking irony was just an accident. Either way, I couldn't shake the memory of Michael's hands over your nose and mouth.

I tried to relax, to prepare myself for the visit, but I couldn't help picturing all sorts of scenarios in my mind. In one, I saw myself standing by Michael's bedside. He gave me that evil grin, then reached under his pillow for a gun and shot me straight in the head.

I tried to find a mantra to calm myself down, and went to pull an outfit together for the visit.

I decided on a simple black top with a pullover teal sweater, and fitted jeans, tucked into long black boots. It wasn't what I'd wear to church or court, of course, but it seemed appropriate for seeing Michael. I accessorized with a simple sterling silver necklace, a few sterling silver bangle bracelets, and my wedding ring.

I looked down at my white gold engagement ring, which had been reset as a gift for our ten year wedding anniversary. Nick had bought new smaller diamonds and had them set around the original 1.5 carat diamond. The jeweler had taken his time with the redesign, so I was without my ring until just after our eleventh anniversary. Eleven. The walls echoed a child's voice: *You know I died when I was eleven.*

I glanced at my watch and saw that I had enough time to give my ring a good cleaning. In a few minutes I had it spotless, and I slipped it back onto my ring finger where it belonged. The diamond sparkled under the pink vanity lights. I now had the strength to meet with Michael face to face.

When we arrived at the hospital, we were told that Nick would have to remain in the regular waiting room near the elevators. He wasn't on the immediate visitor list, and with Michael under close police guard and in critical care, there were no exceptions.

"Don't worry, I'll be fine. Just knowing you're here is support enough," I said with a smile.

"Maybe for you, but I'd prefer to be there," Nick replied. He gave me a kiss for luck and sat down.

I headed down the corridor which led to Michael's room. Sadie greeted me in the hallway.

"Jean, I'm going to be right outside the door in this chair. If you upset my husband, I'll ask you to leave," she said.

"I understand."

"Just so you're aware, he's been formally charged with Carl's murder, but he hasn't met with his lawyer yet. He's not stable enough to move to another facility."

"Thank you for letting me know. Can I go in now?"

Sadie simply nodded and stepped aside.

The police officer on guard opened the door and ushered me inside. Michael was lying on his back, staring at the ceiling. A halo was screwed into his head, keeping him from turning toward me, but he watched me through the corner of his eyes. Then he blinked hard and looked back at the ceiling.

"Do you believe in God, Jean?" His voice was raspy, and just barely audible. "I always wanted to, but I couldn't. Not until the instant that bullet went into my body." A tear leaked out of the corner of his eye.

"Yes, Michael, I believe in God." I could feel tears forming in my own eyes.

"I thought so. You went to Sunday school every week."

"Yes, I did."

"My parents never made me. We're Catholic, you know. It's a sin to skip Mass."

"Maybe you should be talking to a priest instead of me."

"What, for last rites? Confess a few sins? Ask for absolution?" Michael choked a bit as he tried to laugh.

"No, just to talk. Maybe a priest could help you sort things out."

"Maybe. But I need to be talking to you right now. Jean, I never thought God could care about someone like me until the moment I held that gun to my chest and pulled the trigger."

"So why are you telling me this?"

He sighed and coughed a little bit more. "I was wrong to send you that letter. I had it all wrong." He squeezed his eyes shut and more tears streamed down his face.

I waited a few seconds then said, "Michael, I'm glad you believe you found God."

He opened his eyes. "Jean, in the moments before I pulled that trigger, I was filled with the worst anger I've ever felt. But the instant the bullet hit me, the anger was gone and I felt only peace."

"So you got a message from God when you shot yourself, but not when you pulled the trigger to murder Carl?"

He ignored my sarcasm. "I guess maybe God was always there inside me. He took away the anger and the pain from the bullet."

"Look, I think it's great that you suddenly believe in God, but maybe the lack of pain was you going into shock. Along with, oh, I don't know, severing your spinal cord?"

"And you call yourself a Christian?"

"OK, you're right. Fine. God does work in mysterious ways."

"I took a life, this time on purpose, and God appeared. Who would have bet money on that happening?"

"God doesn't gamble, Michael."

"No, I guess he doesn't." He stared at the ceiling for a few seconds to collect his thoughts. "You know, the first time I met

Cassie Bellows, it was at Lance House. She came to preach at me and save my soul."

"She was a kind woman."

"Yeah, yeah, I get that. Anyway, she told me about a man who persecuted Christ's followers. She told me that Jesus blinded him for a few days, before his sight was restored. God forgave him and even changed his name when he became a believer. He went on to preach about Him. But in the end, he went to jail and died there still preaching. He's remembered in the Bible for all the good he did, not the bad."

"Yes, Michael. It's the story of Saul, who became the Apostle Paul."

"Paul? That's interesting," he laughed.

"How is that funny?" I asked.

"My middle name's Paul."

My heart skipped a beat. "I guess I knew that, but I'd forgotten."

"Now I think Cassie told me the story because she wanted it to become my story. In an odd way, it did. To believe in God, I was paralyzed and not blinded. I'm sure I'll die in prison, too."

I stood there speechless.

A few moments later, he continued, "Jean, did you ever notice how beautiful it is to see chickadees flying among the bare branches of snow-covered bushes? Because I never did, until I sat there on the cold hard bench waiting and waiting for Carl's bus to arrive."

"No, I never have. I'll try to take the time to notice now though."

"Well, it's a beautiful sight."

"I'm sure it is."

"My senses were sharp and clear just before Carl arrived. The air was cold, and it was snowing. I felt all of the snowflakes as they landed on my face and hands. When they melted, the cold water kind of stung. The wetness seeped through my jeans. At that moment, I think something was telling me that I would never experience those sensations again."

"Michael, forgive me for this, but I have to ask. Why on earth did you shoot yourself in the chest? You had to know that there was a chance you would survive."

Michael laughed. "There you go Jean, always the practical one. You would have liked a more statistically efficient suicide. But really, on one level you have to be thrilled that I am going to rot away in jail, paralyzed and alone. No, in the long run I think you may be more satisfied that I didn't take the coward's way out."

"You are a lot of things, Michael, but I never saw you as a coward."

"Like our little friend, Timmy, when he peed his pants in the woods?"

"Your colors ran true that day, Michael."

"Jean, if I'd handed you the gun, you'd have been happy to shoot me right through the heart."

"You're wrong, Michael. I could never kill anyone in cold blood, not even a man I hate as much as I hate you. If you held a gun to my head and told me I had to shoot you first or die, I still couldn't pull the trigger. That's what separates me from you, I guess."

"Sometimes our actions can be weapons, too, and just as deadly as guns. No Jean, as much as you hate to admit it, you're not that much different from me."

It was as if he had stabbed me through the heart. I couldn't find any words, so I simply stood there silently until he continued.

"So here's how it happened. As soon as I had all the information about Elle, I arranged to visit Carl in prison. As his stepdaughter's half-brother, I managed to get through all the red tape. In the end, he had to agree to the visit, and I was a little bit surprised that he did."

"Big mistake on his part."

"Yes, I guess it was. It's funny, but I think maybe he wanted to see if it would be as easy to hurt me as it was to hurt Elle. So we sat across a conference table in a big room with other prisoners and their guests. Kind of like the visitation lounge at Lance House. Ever been in prison, Jean?"

"You know I haven't."

He just smiled. "He told me all about Elle, you know. He wanted me to understand what happened that night. He told me that it was her fault, really, that she should have known better than to walk around the house looking and smelling so good. It seems that after a few drinks he just couldn't help himself any more. Not his fault at all."

I felt ill. "That's horrible. But it still doesn't excuse what you did. He paid for his crimes in prison."

"What is enough to compensate for a life destroyed, Jean? What would be a fair price to pay?" I didn't answer, so he went on. "And then he told me that he was about to be released. Turns out he got time off his sentence for good behavior. Isn't that nice? I think it's wonderful that he was a good prisoner. Then he told me that he would be coming to live with an uncle not too far from Graytown."

"Another big mistake. Why would he tell you that?"

"I think he meant to intimidate me. Maybe he thought I'd be frightened that he would be living so close to my family. At least that's what I wanted him to think."

"Is that when you decided to kill him?"

"That's when the idea started to form. I had a little less than two weeks to work out all the details. The trickiest part was to figure out exactly which bus he would be taking."

"How did you do that?"

"I tracked down his uncle, called him up, and told him that I was a friend of Carl's from prison. The uncle is wheelchair-bound, so it was pretty easy to talk him into letting me pick Carl up from the bus stop."

"Where did you get the gun? With your record, it seems like it would be hard to buy one."

"Not as hard as you might think. But I stole this one from a friend. It was just easier that way."

"Then you just set up an ambush?"

"I got there early and sat there on the bench for a few hours, drinking whiskey out of a Styrofoam cup." Michael smiled. "Funny, they tell me that all the whiskey in my blood is one reason I'm still here."

"Were you planning all along to kill yourself?"

"No, I really didn't have a plan for after I took care of Carl."

"So, you were just so guilt-stricken that you decided to pull the trigger on yourself?"

"Someone once told me guilt wasn't in my makeup."

"That's cute, Michael," I replied. There was another pause. After swallowing a few more times, he almost whispered, "Elle's had a harder life than me. It started when she was conceived. Wouldn't you agree?"

I thought about it for a few seconds. "Well, I would say that it started when her adopted father died."

"Maybe so, but it seems to me that all of Damian's children are cursed."

"Bad things happen to good people and to not-so-good people, Michael. I'm not sure that you can believe you're cursed and also believe in God."

"Exactly my point. Now that I believe in God, it changes everything I've believed for my entire life. Better late than never, I suppose."

"I have one more question I want to ask, and I hope you'll answer it honestly," I said.

"Go ahead, fire away. No pun intended."

I ignored his odd joke. "I can understand why you wanted to kill Carl. But God aside, I would have thought you cared enough about your wife not to act on it. It seems selfish of you to put her through all of this."

He smiled. "As always, you have to worry about everyone else. Don't you think my wife should be asking that question?"

"I guess it's none of my business, but I still can't see you as a hero in all this as Sadie does. Truthfully, I see Sadie as just one more victim."

"Well, since you asked nicely and I told you I would answer, I will. I know my wife will have a much better life without me. She deserves to be happy, and I've never been able to give her that."

"So, you don't believe that she loves you?"

"Sadie fell in love with the idea of me when she was seventeen years old, and she married me at nineteen. I'm sixteen years older than her, and she was too young to know any better."

"Well, thank goodness you don't have children to go through all this. I guess Sadie will be the only one who really suffers."

"Don't worry, Jean, I don't plan on making her suffer. I'll file divorce papers. I see how other men look at my wife. She'll have no problem moving on."

"Have you filled Sadie in on this noble plan yet?"

"There you go again. Will you ever learn?"

"You're right. I'm sorry, it's not my place."

"I pray God helps me adjust to my new life. Eventually, I hope God can forgive me. And you too, I suppose."

"Yes, Michael, only God can forgive us for our sins when we confess to Him."

"Well, God's a better man than I am. I'm having a hard time forgiving Carl. And I'm having a hard time forgiving you. You are, after all, the author of this whole sad story." He closed his eyes again. "I'm tired now. Please leave."

"Of course. Goodbye Michael."

He didn't answer, so I turned and walked out of the room.

Sadie was sitting in a black plastic chair just outside the door, sipping a cup of coffee. She stood and looked over my shoulder to check on Michael as the door closed behind me.

In the awkward silence, I looked past Sadie, toward the elevators and the room where I knew Nick was waiting. I was startled to see Marilyn Grainger coming down the hall, wearing a puffy grey winter jacket and black cotton gloves.

Sadie turned to look and said, "Oh good, Michael's mom is here. Now we have the whole cast of characters in one place."

"Well, I'll be going," I said, anxious to avoid the scene I knew was coming.

"Oh no, Jean, please stay a while," said Sadie.

"Really, I have to go. I'm sure you and Mrs. Grainger have things to discuss," I said, as Mrs. Grainger arrived and stood awkwardly between us.

"I insist," said Sadie, grabbing my elbow. "Mother, I'm sure you remember little Jeannie Cartwright? Seriously Jean, I really think you should hear what Michael's mother has to say to the son she abandoned."

All I could think to do was to awkwardly stick my hand out and shake Mrs. Grainger's. "It's been a long time, ma'am," I said.

"Um, hello Jean. I see you're acquainted with my daughter-in-law."

"See, now isn't this cozy?" said Sadie.

A nurse brushed by us and into Michael's room, calling over her shoulder as the door shut, "No visitors right now. I'll be finished in a few minutes."

Sadie looked after the nurse, then turned back to us. "How nice," she said, "That will give us girls a chance to talk." She motioned to two more plastic chairs in the makeshift waiting room outside Michael's door and sat back down in her own. The policeman guarding the door looked at the ceiling and pretended not to be aware of us at all.

"I really can't stay," I said.

"Oh, but you must!" she snapped. "You need to hear what Mother Dear has to say. Maybe you'll understand Michael a little bit better. Maybe you'll even have some compassion for him."

Mrs. Grainger acted as if she hadn't heard Sadie's rant. "Thank you, Sadie, for calling me," she said.

"Ladies, I insist that you sit while we wait."

Mrs. Grainger and I took the other two chairs, and the three of us sat in awkward silence. Sadie still held the Styrofoam coffee cup in her hand, and I couldn't help thinking about Michael with his Styrofoam cup of whiskey, sitting on the bench at the bus stop. There was a bit of good planning to go with a disposable cup. After gunning someone down, you would not want to be worrying about taking care of a ceramic mug during whatever was going to happen next.

The nurse propped the room door open and came out, looking at the notes on her clipboard. "All right, the next visitor can go in," she said. "But don't stay too long. He needs his rest."

Mrs. Grainger stood up and dropped her jacket onto the empty chair. "I'll be brief," she said.

Sadie jumped up and beat her to the door. She called into the room, "Michael, Marilyn is here to see you. I'll be right outside this door. If you decide to send her away, just call me."

As Mrs. Grainger went into the room, Sadie sat back down and stared at me. I wasn't sure what I should do, so I just sat there. With the door propped open, we could hear every word being said inside.

"I hope you'll let me stay and say what I need to say, Michael," said Mrs. Grainger.

"My wife told me you came to visit before. I don't accept any kind of twisted apology from you," Michael said.

"Please, let me explain..."

"There is nothing to explain, Mom. I should never have been born. I think we can all agree that would have been for the best."

"I don't regret having you, Michael. I have always loved you. I just want you to understand you're not to blame. The things I did and the things that Damian and your father did made you who you are and shaped your life. I'm just hoping that I can somehow help you find peace."

"Don't worry, I'll be just fine. But I now choose to disown you all, the same way you disowned me."

"I don't expect you to forgive me overnight. But I promise that I'll be here for you from now on."

"So, you're going to come see me every visiting day? Sit by the prison hospital bed and read me the newspaper?"

"Yes, I will."

"No, you won't. I won't allow it. What you need to do now is leave and forget you ever had a son. That should come naturally to you by now."

"Michael Paul Grainger, I always loved you and always will."

"Of course you do. That's why you chose him over me."

"Well, whether you believe it or not, it's the truth."

"You said your piece. It means nothing now that your husband is six feet below the ground."

"Michael, I'm truly sorry. You know that your father's turning over in his grave knowing I'm here visiting you, and hearing me tell you that despite everything, I love you."

"You mean your husband is turning over in his grave. He's not my father. Or have you forgotten that one major detail?"

"Michael, he was your father and he was a good father to you until that day."

"The day that you chose your husband over your son."

"I have lived with the pain of that every minute since. You know that I had to cut myself off from you, to save my marriage."

"If you had chosen me instead, maybe I wouldn't be lying in this bed." He squeezed his eyes shut and coughed. "I'm tired now. You can show yourself out."

I could hear a sob from Mrs. Grainger. "I'll go, but please know that I'll try to spend the rest of my life making it up to you."

She stood for a few moments in silence, then walked out of the room, crying softly. "Thank you, Sadie," she said as she passed by.

Sadie ignored her and went in to Michael's room.

I was just about to leave when I heard Michael say, "Sadie, I'm sorry you married a monster like me. You're too good to be mixed up in all of this. You should have taken a page out of my parents' book and walked away from me years ago."

"Michael, please stop. Your father was the monster, not you. He kicked you out when you were only sixteen, and he forced your mother to abandon you. You paid for the accident with three years in that juvenile facility. I just think Joseph had a hard time getting over the idea he wasn't your real father. It wasn't your fault."

"Sadie, I haven't been completely honest with you," Michael said.

"What were you not honest about?"

"About that night. I was trying to get a reaction from my father, but I went way too far."

"You told me that you came home drunk and argued with him. Did you assault him?"

"No, and he never hit me."

"Okay, what am I not hearing?"

"He'd forgiven me for Hope's death, but he couldn't get past the rock I picked up afterward."

"Well, that happened when you were eleven years old..."

"No, it was more than that."

"What are you talking about?"

"When I picked up that rock, I knew that Damian was my real father."

"You told me that already, Michael. That doesn't mean you tried to kill your half-sister."

"Sadie, the truth is, I can't be sure if I smashed her head with the rock because I was afraid of being accused of her death, or if I just wanted to make sure she stayed dead."

"How could you even say such a thing?"

"Because I felt a jealous rage as I smashed that rock down on her. And now, I ask myself the same question every day: did I want to kill my sister?"

"You told me that you knew the day she died that she was your sister. How did you find out?"

"I overheard a conversation about my birth certificate. They needed it for something to do with school, and they were concerned that someone would notice that my father was listed as 'unknown.' It must have opened some old wounds, because they got into an argument. I'll always remember his words: "Of anybody you could have chosen, why Damian Marksman? The boy is even starting to look like him!"

"How did your mother respond?"

"She said something about promising to love me as his own. Then he said, 'He's my son, and he always will be. He's a blessing in our lives. Let's leave it at that!"

Sadie's voice softened. "So he did love you," she said.

"I really think he did. Right up until the night I got drunk and told him that I may have killed Hope out of jealousy. When I said that, it was as if I had hit him with a baseball bat. He just kind of stood there, moving his mouth, and I thought maybe he was going to be sick. When he finally could speak, he told me to get out. He told me that I was no longer his son, and that he never wanted to see me again."

"Oh, Michael!"

"Then he ordered my mother to pack me a bag, and told her that if she ever so much as talked to me again, he'd leave her and never look back. Both of us sat and watched her pack. The whole time she was filling my bag I cried, but she never said a word."

"That must have been awful. But your mother had a choice that day and every day since to reach out to you."

"Yes, she did. And that's why I can't forgive her."

"I don't think anyone could blame you for that."

"But my mother did run out the door after me, and she handed me two hundred dollars. She hugged me and told me she loved me. She said she wished she was stronger than she was."

"So she must have felt something for you."

"Ha! If she really loved me, she would have found the strength to fight for me. She would have at least tried. Not once in all those years did she try to save me, try to bring me home."

"Oh Michael," she said again.

"Even after Joseph died, she never tried to find me. She never once reached out to make me feel that I was anything more than the animal who killed his sister."

"Michael, you just have to believe in the good in you. You know that I do. I see a part of you that nobody else has ever known."

Michael's voice lowered to a rasp. "I wish my parents had believed in me. I wish that for just one instant they could have seen me through your eyes."

"So do I, Michael."

There was a long silence, then Michael said, "Can you bring me Cassie's Bible tomorrow?"

"I have the Bible with me now. I'll grab it from my purse."

I heard the footsteps of Michael's nurse coming down the hallway, and decided that I should, as Tom Stoppard said, "Look on every exit as being an entrance somewhere else." The perfect "somewhere else" for me at that moment was home, so I grabbed my coat and purse and took off to where Nick was waiting.

When I walked into the waiting room, he jumped up and gave me a long hug. "Are you all right?" he asked.

"I'll be ok," I said. "Let's go home."

On the way to the car, I took a deep breath of the fresh, cold air. I could almost hear the sounds of a holiday parade in my mind, echoing in the drumbeat of my heels on the faded red and brown brick sidewalk. As we silently drove home, Nick took my hand in his and held it tenderly, resting on the center console.

The next morning, over my first cup of coffee, I found myself trying to remember if there was any time in my childhood when I didn't see Michael as evil. I searched my memory desperately, but nothing came to mind.

Then I thought of searching through old photo albums. I hoped that I might find some pictures of our neighborhood group of kids taken before that tragic day, and maybe get a glimpse of a normal, happy Michael. I had a box of albums taped tightly shut and hidden away on a closet shelf in our bedroom. I think that I had packed them away so well, hoping to muffle any chatter from stories they might tell. Now I needed to hear those stories.

I sat on the bed, carefully cut the tape aside, and opened the first box. My heart began to race as I spread the cardboard flaps and peeked inside. The musty smell of time wafted out, enveloping my sense of smell. I reached in and took out five photo albums and laid them out carefully on the floor. Beneath the books, a small tape recorder rested in the bottom of the box. Next to the recorder was a Ziploc bag filled with tapes.

These were recordings my grandfather and I made when I was about six years old. I had interviewed him and asked questions about his life. And about sailing. Mixed in with these tapes was a blue paint sample. It was the color my grandfather and I had used when we painted the wooden rowboat.

That blue rowboat had long since deteriorated behind the wooden shed at my grandparents' old home.

I picked up the tape recorder and turned it over in my hand. I could remember Michael, back when we were around eight years old, listening to those tapes with me, over and over again. After listening to one of my grandfather's stories on tape, Michael and

I would reenact different storm scenes on an imaginary boat that we'd carefully constructed in the woods directly behind your house. I had completely forgotten the short-lived bond Michael and I once shared.

Michael loved the drama of a storm with crew members being lost at sea, while I never wanted anyone to fall off our imaginary boat or get hurt. Michael insisted that there had to be lots of people who died in our storms.

Then one day while we were riding out a nor'easter, I slipped and fell off the log that represented the deck of our ship and plunged into the imaginary ocean waters below.

Michael shouted at me, "Jean, swim! Swim fast! You cut yourself falling overboard, and the sharks can smell the blood!"

"Michael, let me back up! I didn't mean to slip off," I yelled.

Michael pushed me back down and shouted "It's too late! It's too late! The sharks are eating you! They're eating you!" I finally gave up and went home, crying, with Michael calling after me, "Shark food! So long, shark food!"

I went to my bedroom and rummaged through my drawer to find your friendship bracelet. You had given it back to me, telling me that I should give it to Michael since he was my new best friend. I hadn't even considered giving it to Michael, but I hadn't known what to say to you either.

I found you in your yard, reading a book by the oak tree. "Here Hope, I want you to take this back," I said.

"I can't," you said. "I'm not your best friend anymore."

"Yes you are."

"You spend all your time with Michael."

"I used to like to play boating with him, and you didn't want to. But he's not nice any more, and I don't like playing with him."

"So we really are best friends again?"

"We always were, and we always will be."

You smiled at me and said, "Can you help me put my bracelet back on?"

I looked up and out the bedroom window, and there was the oak tree, staring back at me. I got up and pulled the curtains closed so that it could no longer mock me.

A few weeks later, the phone call took me by surprise. "Jean, it's Sadie," she said. "I'm calling to tell you that Michael has an infection and he's having a hard time fighting it off. It seems to be spreading throughout his system, and the doctors aren't sure he'll pull through." I sensed in her voice that she might silently wish he wouldn't recover.

"My heart goes out to you, but maybe it's for the best," I replied.

She ignored my comment. "He's been asking for you to visit. Will you come back?"

"Sadie, I walked out of there planning to never go back."

"Well, this really could be it. You've lived with guilt and regret most of your life. It's a short window of opportunity. Michael's asking for you and time...well, time is not something he has a lot of."

"Yes, I get that. Look Sadie, you've really caught me off guard here. Truthfully, I'm not sure what I want to do. Tell you what, if I'm not there in an hour, I won't be coming."

There was a long pause, then Sadie said, "Ok," and hung up.

When I called Nick at work, he was not happy. "Are you completely out of your mind?" he said. "Why would you let these people keep doing this to you?"

"Nick, you know how much I've struggled with this. I have to put it to rest, and this may be my last chance."

"I can't get away until after work."

"The way Sadie talked, I may not have that much time. I'll be all right. I promise."

"Let's agree that this will be the final visit. Ever. So, say whatever you need to say to him today, and that is it. You will never make this call to me again."

Michael's biological father had already proven that you should "never say never," especially when you were dealing with a Marksman. Still, it was hard to imagine me ever seeing Michael after this. "Agreed," I said.

When I arrived at the hospital, Sadie was sitting next to Michael's hospital bed, reading a passage from the Bible to him. She stopped and looked up at me without showing the slightest hint of interest.

"Pull up a chair and sit," she said.

As I moved the other chair in the room closer to the bed, she reached down, grasped her husband's hand lightly, and said, "Michael, Jean's here."

Michael tried to open his eyes, and I could see how glassy they were. It was as if his body was in one place and his mind in another. His breathing was shallow, and his voice was weak and raspy.

"Jean, take this," Michael croaked, as he pointed to the open Bible. Sadie closed the tattered Bible and handed it over to me. "Michael, Jean has the Bible," she said.

"Read it. Keep it," he said.

I wasn't sure what to do. "Thank you," I said. I opened the Bible and looked up at Sadie, hoping for a hint, but I couldn't interpret the look on her face. I looked down at the page before me and began to read out loud:

"For he has rescued us from the dominion of darkness and brought us into the Kingdom of the Son he loves, in whom we have redemption, the forgiveness of sins."(Colossians 1:13–14).

Michael was drifting off to sleep, but I thought I heard him mumble, "Amen."

The Bible had been well used by Mrs. Bellows. I recalled that when I was a child, Mrs. Bellows was always opening this Bible and reciting passages from it. In fact, the only time I could remember that she hadn't favored me with scripture from this book was the night she interrupted me at Dead Man's Peak.

This was the first time I actually held her Bible in my hands. As I carefully skimmed through the book, I was amazed at all the highlighted and underlined passages throughout.

Suddenly, Michael's heart rate began to drop on the hospital's vitals monitor. I heard nurses racing down the hallway. They motioned for Sadie and me to leave the room. The medical team quickly went to work evaluating Michael. As we both stood in the hallway, I tried to hand Sadie the Bible.

"Michael wanted you to have it. Please don't insult him by not accepting it," Sadie said. She watched as I slid the Bible into my purse.

More monitors in the hallways screeched, and doctors rushed down the hall and into Michael's room. I turned to look at Sadie and, for a quick moment, I thought I saw a brief flash of relief wash over her face. I stood there and took in the scene around me, not sure if I should leave or stay.

I decided I'd stay with Sadie, since she appeared to have no one. Eventually, the doctors were able to revive Michael, then put him back into an induced coma on life support. A nurse named Cheryl stopped and explained to us that they were going to try to adjust his medications to help him fight off the infection. She told us that everything was stable, and that we should go home and get some rest.

Relief was replaced by exhaustion in Sadie's eyes. As we stood in that hallway, an unspoken dialogue developed between us. We silently gathered our things and headed down the hallway, down the elevator, and out of the hospital. In the parking lot, we simply looked at each other for a few seconds, then headed our separate ways without saying a word. That silence spoke volumes, while old voices and accusations echoed through it.

A few days later, Sadie left a message on my cell phone. I shouldn't have been surprised, but for an odd reason I was. "Jean, it's Sadie. I'm sure you'll be relieved and happy to know that Michael died this morning."

I replayed the message one more time, searching for any sense of relief or happiness. Sadie was right. A huge burden had been lifted from my shoulders, and one of the most destructive forces in my life was gone forever. I should be elated.

Instead, I walked over to the kitchen table, sat down, and began to cry. When the tears poured out, they were like the tears God rained down on Earth, when only Noah's Ark could weather the storm.

Kaleidoscope

Red and orange flames combusting in a fire's light
Small white confirmation dress hauntingly bright
Fall highlights of brown, orange, green, and red
Twisted between the fingers of the one now dead
Revealing dark veins from more than just a bed of leaves
Forgiven through winter songs of brown and white chickadees

Chapter VII

As a writer, I couldn't help thinking of *The Great Gatsby*, when narrator Nick Carraway said about Gatsby, "It was the only compliment I ever gave him, because I disapproved of him from beginning to end." I could credit Michael with the gesture of giving me Mrs. Bellows' Bible as an act of kindness, but that was really the only compliment I could work up for him.

I was oddly saddened by Michael's passing. I had watched him speak his last words, directed to me of all people, and I did appreciate having that Bible. When I opened the front door to my house to bring in the morning paper, I was amazed at how much the temperature had dropped over the past few days. The weather was so cold outside it nearly took my breath away.

The way Michael took your breath away.

I shook my head, trying to shake out that thought, and closed the door against the cold.

This was the day of Michael Grainger's funeral, and maybe today would bring final closure for the chapters containing Michael in my life's story. Nick would not be able to attend with me, but he reluctantly agreed that I should attend the service. Part of me expected to return home to a party, thrown by Nick, to celebrate my true last contact with Michael.

Sadie had scheduled a wake for Michael at a local funeral home. As I got dressed, I wondered who and how many people would show up to honor him. She had purchased a gravesite for him that was not too far from Damian Marksman's.

She had decided against having an elaborate service in addition to the wake. Instead, she had asked Father Adams, who had officiated at Cassie Bellows' funeral, to simply say a few words at the wake and at the cemetery.

There were just three cars in the parking lot of the funeral home when I got there. In the foyer just inside the main door, a small table held a guest book opened for signatures, but I walked by without signing it. I wasn't exactly sure why, but I really did not want to put my name in that book.

The large room that held Michael's casket was almost empty. At the far end was the casket with the lid, to my relief, closed. A single large spray of flowers sat on a stand off to one side. Sadie and Marilyn Grainger stood awkwardly next to the flowers, not speaking to each other, in what amounted to a sad little receiving line.

There were four rows of gray metal chairs set up, but only four people scattered among them. Detective Askew sat alone in the back row, while the lawyer Walter Smith and his nephew Parker Grayson sat together in the second row. Sitting alone in the front row was a strikingly attractive woman in a perfectly-tailored and very expensive-looking black dress. I tried to get a good look at her without drawing her attention, but I had no idea who she was.

I made my way over to where Sadie and Mrs. Grainger stood. Sadie said nothing, and made no move to take my hand when I held it out. I dropped my hand to the side and said, "Sadie, I know you probably don't believe me, but I'm sorry for your loss." The words came out weak and raspy.

She studied my face for a few seconds without any emotion at all, then said, "Thank you."

I stepped over to face Mrs. Grainger, who reached out and took both of my hands in hers. She smiled sweetly and said, "Thank you so much for coming, Jean."

"Mrs. Grainger, I'm also sorry for your loss," I said.

"I appreciate that, Jean," she said. "I really do."

I stood there for a few seconds, desperately trying to think of something else to say. Finally, all I could come up with was, "Well I guess I'll sit down now."

I took a seat in the front row next to the woman I didn't recognize. She looked up and smiled at me as I sat down. "You're Jean Rhodes, aren't you?" she asked.

"Yes, I am" I said. "I'm sorry, but have we met?"

"No we haven't, not yet," she said, "and it's nice to finally meet you. I just wish it hadn't been under these circumstances. My name is Rachael. I'm Elle's stepsister."

I almost gasped. "I'm, uh. I'm sorry for the loss of your father," I said.

"Thank you for that, but my father was a horrible man. I don't think anybody is going to miss him very much."

I had no idea how to respond to that, so I didn't. "So, what brings you here to, ah... to..."

"To the funeral of the man who killed my father?"

"That's not exactly how I was going to put it."

She smiled gracefully. "It's all right. Really it is. There are a number of reasons for me to be here, I suppose, not the least is that I hoped to meet and thank you."

"Thank me? For what?"

"Elle's inheritance, for one thing. That was really sweet of you to seek her out like that. Another person would have been less noble and simply kept the money."

"I wouldn't call it noble. I feel terrible that it wasn't done years ago," I said. "If Elle had known about that money, her life may have been very different."

"We have no way of knowing that," said Rachael. "In fact, I don't think the money would have changed what my father did to her at all."

I looked at her in disbelief. "You really don't blame me for any of this?"

Rachael smiled. "Of course I don't. And I also want to thank you for bringing Michael into our lives."

"What? You can't be serious."

"I am serious. Michael was amazingly loving around Elle."

"Are you sure we're talking about the same Michael? I never knew him to be loving around anybody or anything."

"That's a little bit unkind, considering where we are."

"You're right, I'm sorry. But I thought Michael just looked you up so he could track down Carl. I didn't know he met Elle in person."

"He certainly did meet her. You would have thought they grew up together, and he really seemed to understand the fact that she is a child in a woman's body. They played tea party, and he sang nursery rhymes with her. He cried when he met her, and again when he had to leave."

"Michael? I had no idea."

"Elle is partially aphasic, especially when she is upset or around people she doesn't know so she has trouble with some words. She couldn't handle 'Michael,' so she called him 'Mike.' He told her it had a nice ring to it."

"I never thought about it before, but at no time in our childhood, did anybody ever call him Mike."

"I think it was almost like a new identity for him."

"Rachael, Michael told me that he found God the day he killed Carl and shot himself. It sounds like he might have started that process on the day he met Elle."

"I think you just might be right about that," said Rachael, "and that's the last reason I'm here today – to honor him. It's kind of sad that so few people came."

So here was another woman who saw Michael as a knight in shining armor. "Yes, I guess it is a bit disheartening," I said. "Look, Rachel, in my experience, Michael always came at life from a place of anger and violence, not love. That's the way nearly everyone knew him, and I think the reason there are not more people here today."

Rachel shook her head. "The way I see it, it wasn't anger that led him to murder my father. No, the way I see it, it was love, maybe in one of its purest forms." She paused and looked earnestly into my eyes. "Jean, I'm going to tell you something that may relieve you of some of that guilt you're hanging onto."

"I'm listening," I said.

"You should know that my father was dying of pancreatic cancer, and he had only a few months left to live. Since you didn't know about Michael's visit with Elle, you probably didn't know about his visit with Carl."

I was stunned. "I did know that Michael went to see Carl, but not about the cancer. And how is that supposed to make me feel better? I feel even worse now, knowing that Michael took revenge on a man who was going to die anyway. All this is for nothing."

"I'm sorry, I wasn't clear. He knew that Carl had terminal cancer even before he visited him."

"Excuse me? He knew?"

"Jean, I'm sorry. I didn't mean to upset you."

"I'm shocked. Absolutely shocked."

"I wanted you to understand that it wasn't anger driving Michael. It was his love for Elle. It may have felt like anger inside him, but it was driven out of love."

"Rachael, if Sadie doesn't already know, please keep this to yourself. She doesn't need any more heartache. If Michael really loved his wife, he wouldn't have committed either shooting, especially knowing that Carl was dying."

"Well, I don't know how much Michael might have told Sadie, but I'm not so sure she would see it the way you do. I've seen how deeply Michael could love, and I'm willing to bet she has, too." She reached over and took my hand. "Jean, I'll honor your request to keep this between us. But it really seems that by now you would have learned not to interfere in things like this."

Rachael's words stung, and I realized that I was having trouble leaving the situation up to God. I needed to find a way to hand everything over to Him. "All right, good point," I said. "Rachael please, just do what you think is best."

Rachael smiled at me. "I will," she said.

I felt a need to change the subject. "Rachael, can I ask how you ended up being Elle's caregiver? That's a huge responsibility, and I admire you for it."

"You should send that admiration somewhere else. I'm not a martyr."

"You should learn to take a compliment," I said with a smile.

"Touché. OK, so how it happened is that I was twenty-five when my father hurt Elle, and engaged to be married to a very wealthy man. I knew that Cindy, Elle's mother, couldn't afford all the expenses."

"So, you asked your future husband for financial help?"

"No, I didn't. I insisted that we get a pre-nuptial agreement drawn up to include a section making sure that Elle's medical expenses and on-going care would be covered. Thomas agreed, and never looked back."

"Wow, he sounds like a wonderful man."

"Yes, he is. We even moved up the wedding date. I think the twelve-year age gap between us has been a blessing."

"I guess your life contradicts the old saying that money can't buy happiness."

"Money can help turn a bad situation into a manageable one, Jean, that's all."

"You must have loved Elle a lot."

"Actually, I didn't get that much of a chance to even know her. Elle's mother married my father just a few months before I left home. Elle and I did share a room that last summer."

"You did have a little bit of time to get close."

"She was eager to have a big sister, but unfortunately I kept her at arm's length. I had other things on my mind. And I wasn't all that sure how she and her mother were going to fit into our lives."

I read between the lines as Rachael spoke, and wondered what Carl might have done to her. It seemed likely that she moved out to save herself from him. Maybe she had even known what was happening to Elle, and regretted that she hadn't tried to stop it. In any case, I felt sure that as soon as Rachael moved out, Carl's awful attention must have shifted to Elle. I fought back tears at the thought. "So how does Cindy fit into your life and Elle's now?" I asked.

"Actually, a few months after Elle woke up from the coma, Cindy locked herself in the garage with the car running. She died from carbon monoxide poisoning. It was all too much for her."

"That's so sad."

"Yes it is. I don't think she and Elle were very close in those final few years, because of my father. But after he hurt Elle, Cindy blamed herself for bringing him into their lives. In her defense, he could be very charming and keep his dark side well-hidden."

"Does Elle understand what happened to Cindy?"

"We've tried to explain it to her, but she doesn't seem to understand. I guess there is at least some bright side to the fact that she can't hold a thought for any length of time."

So now I could add Cindy to the list of lives that had been affected by the things I'd done. Looking at Rachael, it also occurred to me that poor Elle had in a sense lost two mothers to suicide and three fathers to early death.

I felt a panic attack coming on, so I excused myself to the ladies room to compose myself. It was time for another dose of Valium, so I broke up a pill and swallowed it with a cupped handful of water from the bathroom faucet. I leaned on the sink and studied my own face in the mirror, waiting for the medication to kick in. Funny, I couldn't find any trace of little Jean Cartwright in the woman who was staring back at me.

I found myself wishing you would appear beside me. Little Hope Marksman would still be there, always there, always eleven years old. Maybe I could explain to you how wrong it felt that I was one of the very few people who turned up to say goodbye to Michael, to smile sympathetically and express my condolences to his wife, a woman who hated me. A woman who in another life could have been my friend.

But you didn't show up, and in a few minutes I felt the cool chemical calm from the Valium take over. I straightened my hair, then returned to the wake and sat back down next to Rachael.

Almost as soon as I was back in my chair, Father Adams began the short service. He took the time to remind us about the Kingdom of Heaven, and told us about Michael's place in it. He reminded us that a place was waiting for all of us in the Kingdom.

I found myself wondering if Father Adams might be mistaken about where Michael would end up. I knew he had been raised Catholic, but I didn't know if he had actually been baptized or if he had received last rites. If he had, and if he believed in the grace of God during his final days, he would be one of God's beloved.

Back in my car after the service, I entertained the idea of skipping the graveside ceremony and simply driving home. Something compelled me, though, to join the rear of the line of cars behind the hearse carrying Michael to the cemetery.

Our little procession rolled through the elegant granite archway entrance to Ansel Cemetery and past the two oak trees standing guard over the road. A light dusting of snow covered their bare branches, and I thought that these graveyard sentinels were somehow less threatening than the tree in my backyard.

Walking up the path to the grave, I caught the spiked heel of my left shoe in a frozen rut and nearly fell. A backhoe, certainly the one that had dug Michael's grave, sat a little way up the hill, waiting to cover him with dirt after all of us had gone our ways.

Four men employed by the funeral home carried Michael's simple pine casket from the hearse to the grave. Here was just one more sad detail, the fact that Michael didn't have enough friends to act as pallbearers. That plain casket was strangely fitting for him, and I had a quick vision of Michael running between the pine trees to discover the secrets of Dead Man's Peak.

I stood next to Rachael as Father Adams read some short passages from the Bible and delivered a few more words about Michael. Then Sadie stepped forward and silently placed a single red rose on top of the pine casket - just as she and Michael had done a few months back for Cassie Bellows.

When the service was over, I turned to say good-bye to Rachael, only to find her staring, her mouth open, at the cemetery entrance.

"Rachael, is everything okay?" I asked, gently placing a hand on her shoulder.

She turned to me and smiled. "Yes. I'm just kind of surprised to see an eagle up in that oak tree."

I turned to look, and sure enough there was a bald eagle sitting on a branch halfway up the tree to the left of the arch. "Well, that certainly is a sight you don't see every day," I said.

Rachael looked back to the tree with a faint smile. "It reminds me of a sermon Elle and I heard in church, a very long time ago. It was based on Soren Kierkegaard's fable of the eagle and the goose."

"I've not heard it."

"It was about a case of mistaken identity. It seems that a young boy found an eagle egg and put it under the goose in the barn, and the goose raised the eagle as one of her own. As the young eagle grew, he looked different than the young geese. This made him very unhappy, and he felt like an outcast. Then, one day when the young birds learned to fly, the eagle discovered that rather than flapping like a goose, he could soar like an eagle, which is what he was always meant to do."

"What a wonderful story."

"The sermon was about baptism, and how we simply need to be what God intended us to be. The minister said that we are all God's beloved. Somehow that sermon always stayed with me."

"I can see why."

"Elle said afterward that she felt like she was like that eagle egg. She knew she was adopted, and she felt she was destined to be more. On the way home after the sermon, she told me that she was waiting and believing. Of course, that was before..." Rachael's voice trailed off. "Well, enough about that."

We both stared silently in the direction of the tree. While we were hearing the story, the eagle had flown away. Rachael was first to break the silence. "Look Jean, I'm sorry we met under these circumstances. I really want to wish you and your family all of God's blessings."

"Thank you, Rachael, and same to you and your family."

Rachael looked thoughtfully into my eyes. "Jean, you're an eagle, you know. Not a goose. Start living like one."

I just smiled and said, "Thank you."

As I headed back to my car, a cold breeze swept through the air. A fine powder of snow blew off the tree branches and swirled around my head, and a cold shiver ran from my head to my feet. Back behind the wheel with the motor running and hot air blowing from the vents all around me, I couldn't bring myself to drive away. I just sat there and waited until all the other cars had left. Then I took a few deep breaths, shut off the engine, and got back out of the car.

As I walked back up toward Michael's grave, I could see that the workers had already lowered the casket, and the man on the backhoe was busy covering it with dirt. I circled around up the hill a bit, so I could watch from a distance.

Listening to the roar of the backhoe and the sound of dirt falling into the grave, I discovered that I had no tears left for this moment. I had spent them all the day Sadie's voice mail told me that he was gone. Now Michael was that brown avalanche, and I wondered if it would finally serve to suffocate the evil side of him that I could not seem to let go of.

By the time the grave was nearly full the cold was starting to get to me, so I rubbed my hands together and stamped my feet. I looked down and saw that I was standing in front of a gravestone with a familiar name on it. It read, "Katrina Margaret Copeland 1975–1993."

Katrina. Our friend Katie. She was there on the day you died. A deep chill went through my body.

I'd almost forgotten about Katie. Even though we had been close friends, we hadn't seen much of each other after the accident, and I had not made any effort to keep in touch with her after we moved away. It had never occurred to me to try to contact her when I moved back.

I read the marker again. If she died in 1993, that would have been our senior year in high school. I felt a flood of regret that Katie had so thoroughly drifted out of my life that I didn't even know that she was gone.

And I had completely forgotten that Katie's middle name was Margaret.

Katie and I had met up on the street behind my house with our sidewalk chalk to draw the lines for the four square game. More of our friends would be joining us soon, but Katie and I liked to be prepared.

Danny's little sister, JoAnn, came bounding out through the glass storm door of their house with her two lopsided ponytails flopping behind her. When she spotted me and Katie in the road in front of her house, she ran over to us and said an enthusiastic, "Hello! Can I play?"

"Sorry, JoAnn, but we're getting this ready for the big kids," said Katie.

"Ok," she said, "then I'll play hopscotch. Can I borrow your chalk?"

"Sorry," I said, "But we're using it. Why don't you find yourself a rock or something?"

"Ok, I will," said JoAnn, and she skipped off to search for the perfect stone. JoAnn was several years younger than we were, and she was always relentlessly happy.

After we finished our four square box, Katie and I sat on the grass at the edge of the road and pretended to watch JoAnn singing to herself and playing hopscotch. The cool dampness of the grass seeped through my jeans as I picked a single, lonely yellow buttercup and twisted it absently in my fingers. "It's like we've been friends forever, and I don't actually know," I said. "Is Katie your real name, or is it Katherine?"

"Neither,"said Katie."It's Katrina. Katrina Margaret Copeland."

"Katrina," I said, trying out the cadence. "Katrina. I love that name. If I were you I'd be Katrina all the time. And I could be Margaret."

Katie giggled. "What's wrong with Jean?"

"Jean is boring. Just 'plain old Jean.' But Margaret sounds like a great poet. We could be 'Katrina and Margaret!'"

Katie laughed again. "Well, I like Jean just fine," she said, "and I like being Katie."

"Ok, you win," I said. "Still, 'Katrina and Margaret...'"

I still loved the name Margaret. I had given it to my daughter, without consciously knowing that it was a kind of tribute to Katie.

It appeared as if no one had paid any attention to Katie's grave in years. Weeds, dead leaves, and a torn candy wrapper were piled up around the headstone, and a light crust of dirt caked the letters of her name. I took off my gloves, and with Katie's warm giggle echoing in my memory, I got down on my knees and did the best I could to clean it up.

Back in the car, I looked at my hands on the steering wheel, covered with grime from Katie's grave, and resolved to get on the Internet to find out how she died.

As I drove through the arch and out of the cemetery, I noticed the eagle soaring overhead. He performed one majestic loop directly overhead, then with a flip of his wings disappeared in the distance.

Turning down High Street toward the center of town, the skies darkened and a few snowflakes began to fall and melt as they landed on the windshield.

My online search was disappointing. I only got one hit, a brief article about a memorial fundraiser held in memory of Katrina Margaret Copeland. According to the article, Katie had been killed in a tragic car accident, involving drinking and driving by a group of teenagers. The fundraiser was to raise money for SADD, Students Against Drunk Driving. Even though I'd only located the single article, I knew that every back issue of the town paper was archived on microfilm at the public library.

I called to my daughter as I headed out the door, "Meg, I need to go to the library for a few hours to do some research. Can you please take the lasagna from the fridge and put it in the oven around five tonight? The instructions are taped to the tin foil."

Scrolling through microfilm, I located more articles that filled in the details of Katie's death. I sat there and silently wept as I read that she had been riding in a car with four other teenagers. The driver was a boy named Richard Darksham, who was two years older than us. He, his girlfriend, Nicole Smith, and her friend, Michelle Parker, all had alcohol in their systems. The other two passengers, another pair of high school sweethearts, were Katie and Daniel Eckleberg – our friend Danny.

The accident had happened not too far from our development. The car had gone off the road and flipped several times before hitting a tree. The EMT crew had used the Jaws of Life to extract all the passengers from the car. Four out of the five kids in the car had sustained serious injuries, but were expected to make full recoveries. Katie was not so lucky, and was pronounced dead at the scene.

I searched through the microfilm, then on the Internet, for any other information about Danny. The only other mention of his name I could find was the obituary of his mother, dated when Danny would have been almost eighteen. On the way home, I looped a little bit farther down the street and drove past Danny's old house. A carved sign over the garage read, "The Allans."

Later, while Meg and Nick talked over dinner, I was lost in thought. I wondered if the impact of your death had played any role in Danny and Katie getting together later and dating in high school. I could imagine how the night of that crash and losing Katie must have affected him, especially since he lost his mother at about the same time.

After dinner, I continued my search for Danny on Facebook, but I was still unable to locate him. I was, however, able to locate Danny's younger sister, JoAnn. She had included her maiden name, Eckleburg, in her Facebook page, and I recognized some of the names in her friends' list. After staring at JoAnn's profile for a few minutes, I sent her a brief message. I asked if she was the sister of Danny Eckleburg, and if she remembered me from our neighborhood. I asked if she could give me any contact information for Danny.

She responded almost immediately, saying that yes, she was Danny's younger sister and, of course, she remembered who I was. Instead of providing me with Danny's contact information, she asked me to meet with her in person, Saturday afternoon at the café next to the RRK indoor ice rink across town. She said that her daughter had a figure skating lesson, and we could talk over a hot chocolate. I accepted the invitation, and counted down the hours until Saturday afternoon.

As I parked my car in the parking lot, I noticed how the sun was shining through the trees surrounding the ice rink and café. I sat in my car for a few extra minutes and watched as parents and children piled out of their cars and headed into the arena, then I turned off the engine and walked into the small café. I was a few minutes early, so I seated myself at a small table in the back, facing the door.

I was absently gazing at the simple paper menu when I heard the café door open and looked up to see the unmistakable smiling face of JoAnn. "Jean, I'm so glad you reached out to me," she said.

"Thank you for taking the time to meet with me in person."

JoAnn took off her bulky jacket and draped it on the back of her chair. I was a little bit startled to see that she looked as if she were at least eight months pregnant.

"I'm thrilled you could meet up with me, Jean. My husband will be here soon to pick up my daughter, so we can spend some time catching up."

"Wonderful! Be sure to thank him for me," I replied.

"Actually, you can thank him yourself. The lesson's almost over and he'll pop in to say hi before leaving."

We had just settled back with our heavy ceramic cups of hot chocolate, topped with whipped cream, when the door opened and a tall man walked in, followed by a young girl whose explosive smile told me that she could only be JoAnn's daughter.

"Jean, I'd like you to meet my husband, Eric, and my daughter, Bree." JoAnn gave the little girl a hug. "So, how did the lesson go?"

"Super! I'm going to be in the Olympics!"

"Maybe you'd better learn to skate backward first," said Eric. "Pleased to meet you, Jean."

"Mommy, can I have some hot chocolate?"

"You can have a sip of mine, then Daddy is going to take you home."

Bree tried hard to set her face in a pout, but Eric said, "On the way home, we'll pick up a pizza for lunch."

Bree brightened up immediately. "Yay! Double cheese?"

"Well, ok," said Eric, "since you're going to be in the Olympics."

"Yay! Bye Mommy. Nice meeting you, Mrs..."

"Jean."

"Mrs. Jean!"

As we watched Eric and Bree leave the café, I said, "JoAnn, she is just as adorable as you were."

JoAnn laughed. "I'm not so sure my brother and the rest of you guys thought so."

"I guess we were pretty mean to you sometimes."

"You know, I thought you big kids were the coolest people in the world. I wanted to be Hope and Jean."

I took a sip of my hot chocolate. "I'm sorry that Hope and Jean didn't work out so well."

JoAnn stroked the side of her cup. "I guess not. So what made you start searching for Danny after all these years?"

"Michael Grainger just died."

"I know. It was in the paper. He was the only one of Danny's friends who really scared me."

"I think he scared all of us. Anyway, his funeral was last week, and while I was at the cemetery I ran across Katie's grave. I didn't know that she was..." I felt a lump rising in my throat.

"You didn't know about the accident? No, you moved to another state. How could you have known?"

"Well, I feel like I should have. Anyway, I did some research and got all the basic facts. I have to confess that it broke my heart when I learned that he and Katie had been dating."

"Yes, they went out for a few years. The sad thing about it all is that Danny felt like he should have been driving that car. He and Katie were the only ones who had not had anything to drink. He even offered, but it turned out that it was a stick shift and he had only learned to drive an automatic."

"Poor Danny."

"It gets worse. He also blamed himself that he didn't call our mother or Katie's parents for a ride. They knew that Richard was drunk, but they were afraid to cause trouble. Danny felt like it was his fault that they even got in that car."

"Oh, JoAnn, that's horrible."

JoAnn gave a little chuckle and a wry smile. "Do you know, when he was in the hospital after the accident, Danny made me promise that I would learn to drive a stick shift. And, that if I ever had any children, I'd do the same for them."

I couldn't suppress a smile. "Danny was always the sweetest guy," I said. I took another sip from my cup and paused for a while. "JoAnn, you know that Danny and Katie were with us the day Hope died."

"I know. It seems like we all cried for weeks."

"I have never been able to forgive Michael for what happened that day, but I've also had a hard time forgiving myself. I can't help wondering if Danny and Katie blamed me. Did he ever talk about it?"

JoAnn reached across the table and covered my hand with hers. "Jean, I can promise you that neither of them blamed you."

"Thank you for that. So where is Danny now? I'd love to talk to him, if you can help me get in touch with him."

JoAnn moved her hand back to her cup. "That's a difficult question. The truth is, I don't have any idea where to find Danny."

"What? What happened?"

"That's kind of a long story. First off, a couple of years after you moved away, our parents got divorced. In fact, Dad divorced the whole family."

"Seriously? It seems like he was always so involved with you and Danny. I never heard them argue."

"They never did. As far as we knew, everything was fine. Then, one day he just announced that he was leaving to start a new life. He served papers asking my mother for a divorce, and said that there was another woman he was going to marry. A month later we found out that his new woman had a baby, and that I had a new half-brother. And once the divorce was final, we never heard from my father again."

"Not at all?"

"Well, after the accident, when Danny was in the hospital, our father sent him a card."

"You're joking."

"I wish I were. And the pathetic part is that Danny treasured that card. He was in the hospital for more than three months, and I think it actually helped him with his recovery. He apparently saw some sort of power in it. Of course, the rest of us were angry that our father never bothered to call or visit Danny."

"Oh, JoAnn, I'm so sorry. I mean that truly from the bottom of my heart. So you have no contact with your father?"

"No, he cut himself off completely. To be honest, I'm not even sure how many half-siblings I have."

"I don't know what to say. Do you know what was on the card your father sent Danny?"

"No, he never let anyone else read it. But whatever Danny saw on that card didn't last long. One morning, I found it ripped into pieces on the top of the trash bucket in the bathroom. Not too long after that, Mom was diagnosed with cancer."

"Yes, I was sorry to read your mother's obituary. I'm sure it was tough, and my heart goes out to you."

"Thank you. It still makes me sad that my mother never met her grandchildren. But I've talked about her so much that I know they have an idea of the wonderful woman she was."

"Yes, it's important for them to feel a connection to her. And from what I've seen of you as a mother, you've learned a lot from her."

"Thank you, that's kind of you."

"I just call it as I see it."

"So about two months after Danny got out of the hospital, we found out about Mom's cancer. Danny was only eighteen, but the burden fell on him. He cared for her through the whole ordeal, and he never once complained."

"You both were so young," I said.

"Yes we were. It was a fast-moving cancer, and Mom passed away just three weeks after Danny turned nineteen. Instead of going to college as he'd planned, he stayed home and took care of me."

"So your brother had to become your father."

"In a sense he had to. Both Danny and I skipped early adulthood. Eric and I got pregnant when we were still in our senior year of high school. Our Sammy was born a week after we graduated, and Eric and I moved in with his parents. Now Sammy is seventeen and about to graduate high school himself."

"So what did Danny do after you moved out?"

"He sold the house just before Sammy's first birthday. He came to the birthday party, but the next day he packed up and left. On his way out of town, he let himself into my house and left a card for me on the foyer table. In the card was a handwritten note. It said, 'I love you more than you will ever know, but I just have to get as far away from here as possible. Please don't try to find or contact me.' There was also a check for $20,000. I assume it was from the sale of the house."

"Again, I don't know what to say. And you haven't heard from him since?"

"About six years ago, I received in the mail a book on the law of attraction, along with a handwritten note. I memorized the note and recite in my mind all the time. Danny told me to not just settle for the role of mother and wife, but to connect with the person I am on the inside and to attract the life I want to live. He said, "This book will help you create the life you deserve. And remember I'm with you always. I love you. You're the spitting image of our mother, a guiding angel above. One of these days we'll meet again.'"

"That's wonderful. Did you notice the state it was mailed from?"

"I did notice the state, but I've respected his wishes not to try to locate him."

"I'm not sure I could do that. And no word from him since then?"

"No, nothing. But I've read that book from cover to cover, over and over again. I've worked to be the person I should be. And I'm sure Danny is working at walking the same path, in his own way. It's hard for me to understand why he feels he has to do it on his own, away from me and this place."

"He must have his reasons. A lot of things have happened to him that would be hard for anyone to deal with."

"The sad thing is that Danny didn't get to watch Sammy grow up, and he never even met Bree. And as you can see, I have another one on the way." JoAnn reached down and lovingly stroked her pregnant belly.

"Yes, congratulations! Do you know what you're having yet?"

"Yes, a boy. And we're naming him Daniel after my brother."

I smiled and reached across to take her hand in mine. "Daniel's a great name. And I know that when Danny does return someday, having a namesake will mean a lot to him."

"I hope so." She gave my hand a little squeeze. "Jean, I miss my brother so much. I just pray that Danny has found a way to forgive himself, and to leave the past in the past."

"That's a perfect prayer."

"The book he sent me talks about how positive thoughts attract positive outcomes, while negative thoughts attract negative ones. True peace and happiness come when we hold onto high-energy thoughts, and work to truly appreciate the positive aspects of the world around us."

"What a wonderful message. Actually, the Bible says pretty much the same thing, as in, 'You reap what you sow.'"

JoAnn smiled. "Yes, it does. I think it's only natural for us as Christians to bring our beliefs to this idea of the law of attraction. After all, God is the center of the universe." She stroked her stomach soothingly again.

"It sounds like you've found peace from it all."

"Yes, I have." She smiled again. "It's funny that you reached out to me right now. I've been dreaming of my brother almost every night for the past few months. In my dreams, he's safe and happy wherever he is. Maybe my dream vibrations attracted you to contact me, so I could help you to make peace with yourself. I don't believe in coincidences anymore."

"If I didn't know any better, I'd say you're a mind reader. I am having a hard time finding peace."

"If it helps, I know for sure that Danny never blamed you for what happened to Hope."

I felt that lump in my throat again and fought back the tears. "It does help."

"Bree and I have been reading Peter Pan, the original J.M. Barrie book, and one line in it jumped out at me. It said, '...the moment you doubt whether you can fly, you cease forever to be able to do it.' Of course, that means that the opposite is also true, that in a sense you can fly simply because you believe you can."

"I never thought of it that way."

"Jean, try to let go of your past, and affirm the life you want. Regret, guilt, recrimination, and doubt are all on the wrong side of the emotional scale. You need to believe in inner peace to find it."

Grace

A prophesized Biblical annual pageant
A charming child's tea party imagined
An undisclosed agreement for a trial explained
A divine intervention masking pain
Adoption propriety papers signed
Along with a sealed final will blue lined
A mealtime blessing answered by
The emergence of a fluttering butterfly

Chapter VIII

I sat at the kitchen table looking at my laptop as my daughter studied her own screen across from me.

"Mom, I hope I get into Plymouth State like you and Dad did. And before you say anything, yes, I'll still look at other schools. Oh, and in case you didn't know, it's a university now, not a college."

I felt a twinge of sadness in my heart as it dawned on me how old my daughter was. She was in her junior year of high school and already looking ahead at applying to colleges.

"Mom, did you hear me? I said I really want to go to your college. I thought that might at least get a little smile out of you."

"Sorry, Meg, my mind was on the chapter I'm working on." I sat back in my chair. "Look, it's completely your decision. Plymouth State was great for us, but you need to make sure it's the right fit for you."

"Ok, so how about if you help me with my college application essay. Nothing says I can't get a little help from a professional."

"Sure, honey. Just send it to the printer in my office, and, I'll take a look at it."

But my mind wasn't on my work as I walked down the short hallway to my office; it was on Katie. How many colleges did she apply to? How many campus visits had she gone on? How real were her dreams before the night she died in that car? Since my chat with JoAnn, I had been thinking a lot about Katie.

As I listened to the printer churning out Meg's essay, I couldn't help smiling at the memory of little Katie sitting at the kitchen table in our old house, playing "Secretary-typist" on my mother's ancient manual typewriter, smashing the keys down as hard and fast as she could.

When I got back to the kitchen table with the essay in one hand and a red pen in the other, Meg changed the topic entirely. "So, Mom, can we go out driving tomorrow? I want to do the test again and get my license."

"Maybe Dad will take you. I have to write all day tomorrow. Besides, I don't think you're quite ready yet to retake the exam."

"Mom, how can you say I'm not ready? I barely failed the first time! Here I am getting ready to go to college, and I'm the only one in my group of friends still taking the bus!"

"You are still more than a year away from going to college."

"I wish Lisa didn't live on the other side of town, so she could drive me to school at least."

"The bus is just fine for now, and for the rest of this year."

"Yeah, well once I get my license, I'll drive my friends to school, and anywhere else we want to go."

"Margaret Judith Rhodes, when you get your license, you will not be driving with anyone else in that car except your father or me. And you certainly won't be driving in the dark. Besides, before you take that test again, you need to learn how to drive a stick shift."

"Are you serious, Mom? Do you even hear yourself? A stick? I don't think they even make them anymore!"

"This actually isn't even up for discussion."

"Wait until Dad hears this one!" Meg unplugged her laptop and stormed upstairs.

I took another Valium to help calm me. I had always been protective of Meg, keeping her from playing in the same swampland or climbing the same trees that I had spent hours in as a child. On the day you lost your life beneath the oak tree, I found out that innocence could end without warning. Our friend,

Katie, had lost her entire future when she got in the car with friends who should not have been driving.

I knew that it was unrealistic to think I could lock my daughter up in the house forever. But I could try to keep her safe for just a little while longer.

It was a gorgeous but cold Saturday afternoon, and I wasn't in any state of mind to get any more writing or editing done, so I decided to take inventory on the *Afta-U,* sitting on metal boat stand blocks in the yard, covered with a blue tarp. At the very least, I could check out expiration dates in the medical emergency kit and look over the life preservers to see if any should be replaced.

The boat had been sitting in the yard, under an A-frame shelter of blue tarp, for two years, waiting for us to get started on the restoration work we knew she needed. About the only thing we had accomplished was to change the oil and filter in the engine.

It was chilly out, but I could feel myself sweating in my jacket as I stood on the step ladder and rolled the tarp back. The main deck was just as we'd left it the last time we had the boat uncovered. I walked across the deck, picking up a few oak leaves that had somehow made it under the tarp, and was about to open the hatch to the below-deck living quarters, when I was startled by movement behind me on the ladder.

"There you are," said Nick, still in his business suit, as he stepped onto the boat.

"You almost gave me a heart attack," I said. "Don't sneak up on me like that."

"Sorry. I did call out to you," Nick replied.

"Well, I didn't hear you." I walked over and gave him a kiss. "I think we might need to pick up a few new life preservers before she finally goes back into the water," I said.

"Sure, no problem. Jean, I want to talk about the phone call I got from our daughter. She called me on my cell on the way home."

The Valium was kicking in, and I felt myself sway as if the boat was moving. I hoped my husband wouldn't notice. "Perfect!" I said. "She couldn't even wait to jump all over you when you got home. I really need your support here. We need a united front."

"Jean, did you really tell her she can only drive with us in the car? And that she has to take the bus for the rest of the year? Oh yes, and that she has to learn how to drive a stick shift?"

"Yes, I guess I did. In fact, I think we should all learn to drive a stick."

"Where is all this coming from? A few months ago, you were the calm one taking Meg out for driving lessons. You were the one insisting that we give her the Taurus after she passed her exam."

"I know, but something I learned recently made me change my mind."

"Like what?"

"I learned that Katie and Danny, my friends who were there the day Hope died, were riding in a car with some other kids, and Katie was killed in an accident. It happened in our senior year. Nick, the driver had been drinking."

"Horrible accidents happen every day. We need to trust our daughter not to drink or get in the car with someone who's been drinking. We have had this conversation with her."

"I know it. But Nick, Katie and Danny hadn't been drinking. Danny offered to drive, but he couldn't drive a stick. If he could, she might be alive today."

"Well, I guess that sheds some light on the stick shift thing." Nick put his arms around me. "You can see that your fear is not really rational, can't you?"

"I guess so."

"I'm worried about you. I love you, but you really need to stop letting the ghosts of all these things in the past run all of our lives."

"Of course, you're right."

"How did you hear about Katie's death?"

"I saw her tombstone after Michael's funeral, and I got the rest of the story from Danny's little sister."

"Is there anything else eating away at you that you haven't told me? I thought you'd closed on all that after they buried Michael."

"No, I think I've told you everything."

"You're right, they're irrational. As for that united front, we'll stick with the one we've discussed with her, 'no questions asked,' any time she calls us for a ride home. Right?"

"You're right. I don't like feeling like this you know." A tear trickled down my cheek.

Nick leaned down and gently kissed my lips. "Talk to me. I know somewhere inside is the woman I married. Tell me everything that's on your mind."

During my next visit to the doctor, he changed my medications around and increased the doses I was taking. Meg called them my "happy pills," and she was pretty much right. I found myself walking through life and doing just enough to get by. I watched each day slide by with a kind of detached interest, as if my life were some sort of reality show on television, about a woman pretending to be a mother and wife.

My work began to slide. I would find myself staring at a single word on the computer screen, maybe wondering why a "d" was shaped like that, or trying to remember how you would have pronounced it. I couldn't remember the names of my characters, couldn't imagine how they had come to be there on my computer.

I decided that I'd better concentrate on getting that draft to my publisher, so I devised my own secret treatment plan. I reduced the daily doses of everything by half, except for the Valium - that I cut out completely, except for flat-out anxiety attacks.

Over the weeks I stashed the pills I was not taking in my small suitcase in the bedroom closet. I knew that the cocktail of pills

Dr. Grant had prescribed for me was supposed to help me with my anxiety, guilt, obsessive thoughts and behaviors, and minor depression, yet I hated to take them. So just before my visits with Dr. Grant, I'd stash the unused bottles away, feeling empowered that I'd managed to get through the month on my own terms. After each visit I would come home and fill a glass with Merlot, then sit at the kitchen table, praising myself for being so strong.

And I have to admit that I found some comfort in knowing that I had plenty of "happiness" in reserve, hidden in that suitcase. Just in case.

For a few weeks, I immersed myself in the book. The characters were vivid parts of me and all the people I'd encountered in my lifetime. I willingly jumped onto this emotional rollercoaster, looking forward to the peaks and swoops on the twisting and turning ride.

Then, for the five days leading up to a routine visit with the doctor, I went into what seemed to be an unending anxiety panic attack. For those five days, I started popping the Valium pills twice a day as prescribed, since the sporadic fixes with the Valium were no longer working.

"Dr. Grant," I said, sitting in his office, "you know I'm always reluctant to increase my medication, but this time I'm asking, can we increase the Valium? It doesn't seem to be working like it did before."

"Yes, Jean, based on what you told me about the past week, I do think we should increase the dosage to 10mg. But if you feel that it is a little too strong, please break the pill in half. The pharmacy will have a problem if I call in another 5mg prescription so soon."

I smiled and lied. "Great idea, since I only have a few days left in the old bottle."

I filled the 10mg Valium prescription, and my plan completely changed. I started to take the new dosage of Valium loyally as it was prescribed, twice a day. I also made a large jump up in what I was taking of the other scripts.

One day my publisher called, wondering when the draft I had promised weeks ago would be ready. Luckily, my happy pills were there to mute the disappointment and accusation in her voice. I smiled into the receiver and told her that everything would be just fine. Then I took another pill. I heard your voice whispering in my ear, "*Shhhh. I won't tell.*"

For the next three weeks, I concentrated on writing, but I began to lose control. I found myself taking additional Valium nearly every day. Finally, the rollercoaster jumped the tracks, and I was free falling through the air.

And you were always there in your pure white dress, silently watching. Sometimes I would hear your oh-so-young voice cheering me on as I'd write: *You can do it, Jean!* But when I looked up, you would be just sitting there, silently watching, your expressionless eyes locked with mine.

Finally I got to the point where I didn't even have the energy to write anymore. I only got out of bed to use the restroom or to take a few more pills. *If I can just get a little rest,* I thought, *I'll be able to get it all going again.* So I stayed in bed.

Eventually the idea of taking a shower was more of an effort than I could face, so I just stayed in bed.

Then one evening, Nick sat on the edge of the bed and gave me a gentle kiss on my forehead. "Honey," he said, "I know you're under a ton of pressure. I know you're exhausted and on new medicines, but I'm concerned. Meg and I need you to get up and shower and face each day. We support you one hundred percent, and we don't care if you ever write another word. We just want you back. We love you."

I opened my eyes and looked up at my husband's face. I knew I had to put his fears to rest. I leaned up on one forearm to support myself.

"I don't want you two to worry," I said. "I'll get up and shower right now, then I'll come down for dinner. I'm just feeling out of sorts from the pills." I managed a faint smile.

Once I was in the bathroom, I decided to take a bath instead of a shower. I undressed slowly as the tub filled, looking with horror at myself in the bathroom mirror. My hair was matted and greasy, and my skin looked grey and old. My eyes were watery, with dark circles under them. My naked body looked thin and frail.

I was crying a little bit as I lowered myself into the hot water, the tears streaking the grime on my cheeks. I closed my eyes and took in a deep breath, held it for a few seconds, then slowly exhaled with something between a sigh and a groan. I felt oddly calm and relaxed. I'd feared holding my breath for years, so I decided to hold it for as long as I possibly could. I closed my eyes, sat back, and slid down the white porcelain of the bathtub until my entire head was submerged in the water. I could feel the water washing the tears from my cheeks.

The warmth of the water enfolded me, supported me, caressed me. What a wonderful thing! I could simply go to sleep in this bathtub and just not wake up, and then all my anxieties would fade away for good. Your ghost would fade away for good.

"Oh my God, Jean!" Nick yelled.

I bolted up out of the water in the tub and gasped frantically for air. "Nick you startled me!"

"I startled you? It looks to me like you were trying to drown yourself," Nick said.

"No, I wasn't trying to drown myself. I was trying to wash my hair and you scared the life out of me."

"Jean, there's no suds. I know what I saw."

"Nick, I wasn't trying to hurt myself! Please, don't worry."

"How can I not worry?"

"I know. But still, don't. I promise I'll take better care of myself."

"If not for you, please do it for Meg. And for me." Nick gave me a kiss on the top of my wet hair, then he sat on the closed toilet and chatted about nothing as I finished my bath.

The next few weeks were too hazy for me to recall. On that night after my bath, Nick went downstairs while I was drying my hair, and I took a pill to calm my nerves. Then I took one more to get me through dinner. Then the regular 10mg dose at bedtime.

The days turned into a sort of slow-motion montage of faces and muffled words that I couldn't quite grasp. Sometimes the voice was my own, and still I could not seem to understand what I was saying, or to relate it to anything around me. I would catch sight of you, silently watching, waiting, and I would try to talk to you, but I had no idea what I was trying to say.

And then I found myself lying on my back, my arms strapped down at my sides by a belt across my chest. Fluorescent lights streamed by overhead, and a man's face hovered over mine. He was talking, but the words made no sense at all. With all the concentration I could muster, I could finally make out what he was saying.

"... safe now, Jean. We're going to take good care of you and have you back on your feet in no time."

I struggled against the strap. "Why am I tied down," I asked. "And who are you?"

He laughed. "I'm Dr. Carson," he said. "The strap is just to keep you from falling off the gurney while we get you to your room."

"Where am I?"

"You're in a hospital where we can help you get better. Don't you remember anything?"

I closed my eyes and thought hard. Medicine cabinet. Out of pills. Old bottle of Vicodin from Nick's shoulder surgery. "Oh God," I said. "Did I take Vicodin?"

"Looks like it. We're just going to keep you here for a while until you feel better and you can sort it all out."

"Oh God," I said again. The doctor said something else, but this time I couldn't quite make it out, and I felt myself sliding back into a deep sleep.

I don't remember dreaming, but when I opened my eyes again, I had that panicked feeling you have when you wake up from some kind of nightmare. I looked around the small, stark room with the single window and realized that the nightmare was far from over.

The walls of the room were beige-painted concrete, and the only furniture aside from the bed was a night stand with a plastic cup and a pitcher of water on it, a small dresser, and a straight-backed metal chair. A fluorescent light mounted flush in the smooth ceiling cast a cold greenish light over everything.

I was lying beneath a thin blanket in a narrow bed, wearing nothing but a hospital gown. An IV needle was taped to the back of my hand.

I sat up, swung my legs over the side of the bed, and stood up carefully. My knees felt shaky, and the beige tile floor was frigid to the touch of my feet. I shuffled over to the closed wood-grain metal door and discovered that, as I expected, it was locked.

The other doorway in the room had no door, and it led to a tiny bathroom that had only a simple toilet and a small sink. I turned both knobs on the sink, but only cold water poured out. There was no towel holder, only a roll of paper towels on a shelf by the sink.

I shook my head and laughed. So here I was, in a loony bin. I had once created a character who had been confined to a mental institution, and I learned in my research that you never put a towel rack in a patient's room because she could use it to harm herself.

To harm myself.

There was a door on the back wall of the bathroom, but it was also locked, so I used the toilet and went back to bed.

My stomach was in painful knots, so I pushed the call button tied by its cord to the rail of the bed. In less than a minute, a nurse unlocked the door and came in. I could see through the open door that I was directly across from the nursing station, obviously under close observation. "Well, look who's awake," she said.

I tried to smile. "My stomach hurts. A lot."

"I'm not surprised. They worked it over pretty thoroughly at the urgent care."

"They had to pump my stomach?"

"Um hmm." The nurse stuck the needle into the IV port on the back of my hand. "This should make you feel a little bit better."

"I think I took too much Vicodin."

"That's what your chart says."

"It was an accident. I didn't mean to."

"I'm sure that's true."

"So why is the door locked? Why the suicide watch?"

"Just being careful. You know how it is."

"Sure. I know how it is."

I closed my eyes, and it all came rushing back. My head was pounding with a migraine as I dumped all the pills left in Nick's bottle onto the cutting board and crushed them to powder with a big spoon. It didn't seem like so much when you couldn't count the pills, so I swallowed it all, washing it down with the last of the Merlot in my wine glass.

For some reason it worried me to have all that powder on the cutting board and the spoon, so I put them in the dishwasher and started it up. Then I poured myself another half glass of Merlot, emptying the bottle, and sat down at the kitchen table to stare back at your ghost.

"Ha!" I said. "You don't need pills, do you Hope? You just sit there in that little white dress and accuse me with your eyes. Do you remember pain? Do you remember feeling anything at all?"

And still you stared at me.

"Well, here's to you, Hope. You won't talk to me, and you won't leave me alone." I lifted my glass of wine in a toast.

But before I could take a sip, a moment of crystal clarity took hold of me and I realized what I had done. I could feel my mind separate from my body, hovering over this woman toasting the ghost of the closest friend she would ever have. This woman who was sitting in her kitchen and waiting to die.

But I didn't want to die. Did I? Surely the Vicodin had lost potency. I just wasn't thinking straight when I took it. I wasn't trying to kill myself.

Was I?

And then came a rush of panic. Maybe if I could just vomit up the poison in my system... I tried to get up out of the chair, but I couldn't even stand up. I sank to my knees, clinging to the table. "Help me, Hope," I said. "I can't leave Nick. I can't leave Meg."

But you just stared back at me. And then darkness.

I looked up at the nurse, who was fluffing the pillow around my head. "Who found me?" I asked.

"I beg your pardon?"

"When I overdosed. Did my daughter find me in the kitchen? Or was it my husband?"

"I don't know. We've called to tell them that you're awake. The doctor wants you to stay quiet tonight, then they can see you tomorrow."

"I'm not sure why they would want to see me." For the first time since meeting Nick, I wondered if I'd done irreparable damage to my marriage and my family. I could feel a tear trickling down my cheek. "I've ruined everything we ever had."

The nurse straightened up and smiled. "I'm sure that's not true at all. Your husband was here with you all night, until we made him go home a couple of hours ago. He even left a message for us to give you. He wanted you to know that he and Meg love you, and that they will be here for you."

"He said that?"

"He did. I'd say you were pretty lucky."

"And I can't see them until tomorrow?"

"That sedative that I gave you is going to help you get some rest and start getting your strength back. You won't really be up for much conversation."

"Can you tell whoever needs to know that I haven't been taking the prescribed dosages of any of my medications? Especially the Valium. I was also taking lots of extra pills from old bottles."

"I'll make sure the doctor knows."

As I lay in bed that night, I wandered in and out of sleep. My dreams were vivid and focused on my childhood. In one dream, I was an adult watching Danny at around age seven, pedaling around and around in the dead-end circle, riding on one of our prized neighborhood Big Wheels. The painted silver rim of the front wheel gleamed in the sunlight as Danny pedaled furiously to gain speed, then threw the little back wheels into a sideways spin.

He was wearing one of my father's softball caps. He had a piece of paper taped on the front of it, with a six-pointed star and the letters "CHP" on it. It was a playtime tribute to one of our favorite television shows, *"CHiPs."*

I saw my younger self walking down my driveway carrying an orange plastic gas station pump. Behind the younger Jean was Hope, carrying a small tin box used to collect gas money and tolls. Hope set the box down in the grass next to the driveway and said, "I'll be right back! I'm going to grab some more money!"

Hope went to a nearby tree and gently picked off some leaves officially designated by our neighborhood group as being cash for use in our games. Walking back to the driveway she passed right by my adult self, so that I could breathe in the crisp, clean smell.

From the top of the driveway, another Big Wheel came screeching down and almost knocked my younger self over. It was Michael, wearing a *"CHiPs"* hat like Danny's. There was no anger in his actions, and he was taking his role as "Ponch" very seriously. I could almost see an aura of white light above his head like a halo.

Just then, Timmy came down the driveway on a child-sized bike with training wheels on it, attached so high that they rarely touched the ground. Timmy had a handkerchief tied around his arm just below his short-sleeved t-shirt. These handkerchiefs were tattoos, meant to designate whoever was assigned to play a bad guy for the day.

Katie appeared from around the corner of the house with a red and white handkerchief tied around her arm and carrying a box of Fudgsicles. I laughed as I recalled how on this particular day, when she was supposed to be the other bad guy, she decided to go home and get Fudgsicles.

Katie ran down the driveway to where we were gathered. "Hey, they're melting," she said. "Hurry and take one!"

Michael opened his mouth to scream something, but seemed to change his mind when he saw what gifts Katie had in her hands. My adult self walked over to Katie and took a Fudgsicle to eat. I'd forgotten how great they tasted on a hot summer day.

It had to be mid-summer, and it was scorching outside, with a sun brighter than I've seen in years. I looked over to my mother's rose garden, and saw the rose bushes were in full bloom. I walked over to the rose garden gripping the small fudge-stained wooden stick. The smell of the fresh flowers overwhelmed my senses.

The me in my dream smiled, thinking that even though the people who now lived in my childhood home still kept a beautiful rose garden and I was living right next door, not once in all the years I'd been living there had I stepped over to my neighbor's garden to smell the roses.

I reached down with my free hand to pick a single pink rose. I must have miscalculated where to break it off, because I felt the piercing pain of a thorn digging into my finger. I dropped the rose and instinctively stuck my finger into my mouth to try to stop the bleeding and subdue the pain. I could taste the blood and dirt.

With my finger in my mouth, I turned to look back toward where I'd left the neighborhood kids, but only two remained sitting there. They both were staring blankly at me, Timmy and Danny. Katie, Hope, and Michael were all replaced with their headstone markers from the cemetery. The young Jean was nowhere to be found.

I woke up gasping for air and covered in sweat. My heart was racing and I felt an overwhelming sense of loss. The white halo of light around Michael tormented me. Was it possible that there had been a time when Michael's intentions and heart were pure and innocent?

I wasn't sure why this detail bothered me so much. Here I was sitting in a mental hospital, yet I was fixated on trying to figure out the meaning of the white aura above Michael's head. I wondered when that light might have changed colors.

In the morning a different nurse woke me up. "Good morning," she said, handing me a little paper cup full of pills and a glass of water. "These will make you feel better and not so drowsy. Drink up, then we'll get that needle out of your hand." A stream of light from the window formed a sort of halo around her head.

I looked at the pills. "I think I've been taking too many of these things."

"These are a little bit different from the ones you were on. They'll help you get away from all of those."

I looked into her eyes, then back at the pills. I briefly considered asking her to crush them up, then thought better of it. I picked them one at a time out of the little cup and carefully swallowed them.

As the nurse removed the butterfly IV from my hand, I asked, "What time is it? Do you have any idea when my husband will get here?"

"It's about 7:15 in the morning. Visiting hours start at 9:00."

"Do you suppose I could get a shower before he gets here?"

"Sure. I'll send in the LPN with the key to your shower, and she can help you."

"So that's what that locked door in the bathroom is. You know, I probably don't need help. I've been bathing myself for years."

"Just being careful. You know how it is."

"Yes, I guess I do know how it is."

When Nick arrived later that day, he showed up with six pink roses with the thorns cut off them. "These are from Mrs. Crowley's rose garden," Nick said with a smile. "She asked me yesterday if we'd like some, and I thought I should bring them to you."

It had to be a sign from God, since I'd just dreamt of these exact roses from her garden last night. In all the years we've been neighbors, Mrs. Crowley had never given us any of her roses. I wasn't sure if I believed in coincidences or not, but I did believe in God, and I could see His hand in this.

"Thank you," I said softly. "Will they let me keep them in here?"

"Yes, the doctor cleared them for you to have."

I gazed at the flowers in my hand. "Nick," I said, "please tell me that you found me, and not Meg."

"Yes, I did."

I started to cry. "I'm so sorry. I really didn't plan to put you through all this, and I wasn't trying to kill myself. I just wanted my headache to stop. I wanted the voices to stop."

"And I just want you to get better. Please try not to worry about anything other than getting better and coming home to us."

"So I have a home to come back to? Or is this where you finally leave me and take Meg away?"

"Oh, baby, please don't even think things like that. I love you, but I miss my wife and Meg's mother. I've been beating myself up because I saw all the signs and pretended they weren't there."

"It wasn't your fault at all. I'm a great actress. Perhaps not Academy Award material, but I'm definitely talented." I couldn't help laughing through my sobs.

"From now on, no more acting. And you have to promise you'll never do anything like that again. I know it might be tempting sometimes to try to head home early to God's house, but Meg and I need you here."

"Okay, deal." I dried my eyes on the shoulder of my hospital gown. "I'm glad that's settled."

Dr. Carson tapped on the door to the room. "Mind if I come in?"

"Of course not," said Nick. "Come in."

"Good morning, doctor," I said.

The doctor came in and stood at the foot of my bed. "You gave us a pretty good scare last night."

"I know it. I'm sorry."

"We don't need you to be sorry. We need you to get well."

"As a matter of fact, we were just talking about that," said Nick.

"Good." The doctor stuck his hands in his pockets. "Mrs. Rhodes," he said, "your husband and I had a long talk last night about everything that's happened to you. Then this morning I called your therapist to get a better picture of what's been going on treatment-wise. You've had a very rough time of it."

I felt tears welling up and bit my lip to try to push them back down.

"Jean," said Nick, "Dr. Carson and I think you should stay here a while. At least a few weeks. They can keep better track of you while you get better."

"Do I have a choice?"

"Jean," said Nick, "they won't keep you here without your consent. Meg and I agree that this has to be a voluntary admission."

I smiled at Nick. "Of course I'll consent. Didn't we just make a deal?"

"Yes, we did."

"Just one thing, doctor," I said. "I don't have a problem with spending the next few weeks here, but would it be possible for me to get a room where I don't need a friend with me every time I take a shower?"

Dr. Carson laughed. "Mrs. Rhodes, I think you and I are going to get along just fine. I already have you scheduled to transfer to a room in a more open unit this afternoon, after we get the long-term admission papers signed. Anything else?"

"Nothing I can think of at the moment."

"All right then, I'll look in on you this afternoon in your new room." Dr. Carson headed out and pulled the door closed behind him.

After the doctor left, Nick and I talked about nothing for a while, then I started to feel drowsy. "I guess I'll try to get a couple of hours of work done at the office," he said, standing up. "I'll bring Meg back to see you tonight after dinner."

"That sounds wonderful," I said. "When you come back, would you please bring me a suitcase with some clothes? Oh, and the Bible from the drawer in my nightstand?"

"Of course I will. I didn't realize you had a Bible in the nightstand."

"Yes, I do. Michael gave it to me before he died. It belonged to Cassie Bellows. I've been picking it up and reading it lately, and I find comfort in her notes and highlights."

"I don't know if that's such a good idea, considering the source," said Nick.

"Don't worry, I really feel that it's a good thing."

Nick hesitated. "Ok, I'll try to catch Dr. Carson on the way out. If he thinks it's okay for me to bring you that particular Bible, I'll bring it. But I'd prefer to buy you a new one."

"Fair enough." I kissed him good-bye and was asleep almost before he was out of the room.

That evening Nick and Meg visited me in my new room. It was considerably more cheerful, with a fully-functioning bathroom and shower, three chairs, and even some pictures on the wall. My roses were in a stainless steel pitcher the nurses had found for me.

On the new floor I could wander around pretty much as I wished. There was a recreation room, and a small cafeteria for meals. My medications were stabilizing, and while I felt slightly "fuzzy," I was a lot less drowsy. And I hadn't seen any sign of you.

After Nick and Meg gave me big hugs and kisses, and Meg and I cried a little, Nick opened the suitcase he'd brought and handed me Cassie's Bible. "The doctor said it was fine to give you this. He said it might even help you sort things out."

"Thank you," I said. I tucked the Bible into the drawer on the nightstand.

A few days later, when Nick made his daily visit, he handed me a package. It had been obviously opened and resealed. "The hospital had to open the package and inspect it. I don't want you to think I'd violate your privacy."

I smiled. "I'm so blessed I slipped on that patch of ice in front of that cute boy twenty years ago."

I struggled, trying to tear at the packing tape they had used to reseal the package. Nick chuckled and said, "Here, let me help you."

"As always, my hero," I laughed and handed him the package. He reached over and gently brushed my lips with a kiss, then took the keys out of his pocket and used the house key to tear the tape.

I had been expecting the package to be from my publisher. Instead, I pulled out a handwritten letter from JoAnn, along with a well-used book entitled *The Law of Attraction*.

Dear Jean,

    This is the book Danny sent to me, and it changed my life forever. I like to believe it meant a lot to Danny, too, or else he wouldn't have given it to me. I've read it over and over again, and it's time I shared it with you. Please read it, and try to put the past behind you and heal. And when you're done, when you feel like you understand every word, please go ahead and send it to someone else who might benefit from it.

Best wishes,

JoAnn

The next two weeks felt productive, and I could feel myself getting stronger, both mentally and physically. The therapy sessions involved a lot of tears, but I seemed to come away from each one with new insights. The doctor was gradually readjusting and decreasing my medications, so that "fuzzy" feeling was going away.

I had quite a bit of free time, so I filled it with hours of reading both Cassie Bellows' Bible and the well-loved book JoAnn had given me.

Then, one afternoon, I found myself playing a game of checkers with a fellow patient. I laughed when I recalled my vision, years ago, of Michael playing checkers with another resident at the mental hospital I'd pictured him in.

The only really disturbing things about those weeks in the hospital were the recurring vivid dreams.

In one, Hope and I, at around the age of nine, stared at the plastic ant farm sitting on the small wooden desk in my bedroom. That ant farm had been one of my favorite things, and we had spent many hours watching the ants busily building their tunnels. There were even a few library books about ants on the desk.

The bedroom door behind us was open. Hope turned to look at the young me. "I think it's so cool that ants have two stomachs. One so they can feed themselves, and another so they can share their food with others. I think we can learn a few things from ants sometimes," she said.

The younger Jean gazed at the ants, nodded thoughtfully and said, "I never thought about it like that before."

Hope then started to quietly sing. "This little light of mine, I'm gonna let it shine, let it shine, let it shine, let it shine." I joined her for the second time around, and we just sat there singing and looking at the ants.

When we finished, Hope giggled and said, "I love that song! In CCD, I learned that we're all special because of God's light inside us."

"I just like the song," said the younger Jean.

Michael entered the room undetected and stood behind them. "What are you looking at?" he asked.

We both jumped a bit as we heard him speak, then turned to look at him. Michael moved closer to examine the ant farm.

"You know, I bet miners were kind of like ants. I think it's a tough job, but it could be cool underground mining for something. They don't just mine for gold you know," he said.

"I want to be an archaeologist someday," Jean said.

"So, you want to dig for dead bodies and things?" Michael asked.

Hope came to my defense. "You can dig for things other than bodies, Michael."

"I think it'd be so cool to find dinosaur fossils and old utensils and stuff from the Indians," Jean said.

"What do you want to be, Michael?" Hope asked.

"I want to be an astronaut. I want to find a planet we can all move to if Earth becomes extinct."

"Wow, that's cool!" Hope said.

"So, what about you, Hope? What do you want to be someday?" Jean asked.

"Don't laugh. I just want to be a great wife and mother and live in a nice house and cook, clean, and do gardening."

Michael, of course, laughed.

"Michael, stop. That's nothing to laugh at," Jean scolded.

He stopped. "Hope, don't you want to make a difference in the world and get into the history books or something?"

"I'd be making a difference in my kids' lives, you know," Hope said with a bit of a strain in her voice.

"Well, I'm going to make a difference in this world someday," said Michael.

My adult self, watching all this, felt overwhelmed with emotions and began to cry.

Then the scene changed, and I was no longer in my childhood bedroom. Now this same older self stood near a cliff, waiting for three running children to catch as they ran by. I knew that it was my job, my sacred duty to save them, and I couldn't fail. Like J. D. Salinger's character, Holden Caulfield, in *The Catcher in the Rye*, I was the protector of innocence.

And yet I did fail. As Hope ran past me, I reached out desperately, but I missed her. As she fell backward into the abyss, she looked up at me with that expressionless gaze. Then Michael sprinted by, and again I missed. I could hear him laughing as he fell. Then the young Jean ran up, and this time I managed to grab her hand as she went over the cliff. I held on with silent desperation, looking down into her terrified eyes. Then I woke up, just as she slipped through my grasp and disappeared over the edge.

I woke up crying. Like most of these dreams, it seemed so real that it was hard to shake off. I sat in my room for a long time, staring at the copy of the *Law of Attraction* on my night stand without seeing it, and trying to sort out that dream.

It was painfully obvious that I was still struggling with guilt over failing to save Hope, failing to give her a chance to become a wife and mother. What was less obvious was that insight into Michael, that moment when he saw the world as a place of opportunity, a place where he wanted to make a difference. Sitting there in my hospital room, it became clear to me that all the ambitions and dreams Michael may have had were shattered the day he killed Hope.

At that moment I was able to forgive Michael and myself. I understood at last, and it was from this understanding that my true recovery began.

As the young Hope had pointed out, we're all made in the image of God, but seeing potential and living up to that potential were two distinctly different things. From that moment on, I decided that I'd live up to my potential and take young Michael's advice to make a difference in the world.

A week later, I was released from the hospital. On my first day back home, I was nearly overwhelmed by how toxic that house was for me. Even though you were nowhere to be seen, the sense of sadness hung like a pall over every room, over the yard, even over the garden.

Nick noticed the change in me right away. "Baby, I think we should sell this house and move back to New Hampshire. We could probably even build our dream house if we get a decent price for this place."

"I can write anywhere," I said, "but what about your job?"

"Actually, I have inquiries out and a few great leads in New Hampshire, so I'm not worried about finding a job."

"But it may be too traumatic for Meg to move right now. She's at a vulnerable age, and a change of high school may hurt her, and I couldn't live with that. Maybe we should just sit tight and revisit the idea of moving when she graduates."

Meg had been listening from the other room, and bolted into the living room where Nick and I were talking.

"Mom, I'm good. I think moving to New Hampshire would be awesome! Besides, Grandma and Grandpa aren't getting any younger, and I'd love to move closer to them. Don't worry about me. I'll be fine. So, do I get to design my own bedroom in the new house?"

I laughed and said, "Well, you have both obviously thought this through."

"We've had a few conversations," said Nick.

"Oh, and in-state tuition could be another huge bonus if I end up going to Plymouth State," said Meg. "But I'm still going to live on campus."

Both Nick and I laughed. I said, "All right, so it's unanimous. So where should we go?"

Meg ran into the other room and brought out her laptop. "Let's start looking for places now."

Both Nick and I smiled as we recognized how unselfish our daughter was.

"Okay, so I guess we need to come up with a list of must-haves and wish-we-could-haves," I stated.

We all worked together on a list of "must-haves" and "wish-we-could-haves." We decided we wanted a house on a body of water, with a wooden dock and lots of land, at least two stories, four bedrooms, gas fireplaces in both the living room and master bedroom, a large eat-in kitchen with upgrades, open concept floor plan downstairs, preferably a finished basement or third floor, at least two full bathrooms upstairs, and a half bathroom downstairs.

I reached down and crossed Nick's three-car garage off the list. I felt both of their stares. "I hate garages," I said.

"Seriously?" said Nick.

"Nick, I told you that when we moved here."

"I remember. I just thought the idea of having warm clean cars had grown on you. Who's going to get all the cars brushed and scraped off in the winter?"

"I'm assuming that my knight in shining armor can put on his winter armor and take care of it," I smiled, "Or, we could hire someone."

Nick laughed. "Cute, Jean."

I reached down and added, "Golden Retriever puppy - a.k.a. Attack Dog."

Meg almost squealed, "Oh my God, for real, Mom? You're serious?"

"Surprise!" Both Nick and I belted out at the same time. We both laughed because we had responded as if we'd planned and practiced that same reaction.

"Your dad and I agreed awhile back. We've been on a waiting list with a breeder for a few months now. The mother is being bred shortly, so fingers crossed, hopefully, we'll have a puppy in our new home in a few months," I confessed.

"So is it a male or female we're getting?" Meg inquired.

"We asked for a male so your father wouldn't be outnumbered," I joked.

After a few weeks of searching, we decided on a beautiful three-story, four-bedroom house, on Norman Lane in Meredith, NH. It sat on Lake Winnipesaukee, with not only a dock, but also a boat house. The house was secluded, but not too far from civilization. All three of us agreed that it was the perfect home for our family.

It wasn't very old, but it did require a few renovations. It was just as we all had imagined and more. When we walked through the house, the creative juices began to flow through me, and I could envision myself spending hours here, writing and enjoying the process.

The kitchen was large, with huge windows overlooking the yard and lake. The master bedroom suite was situated on the second floor above the kitchen, and had two walls of windows with magnificent, tranquil views. I felt that the lake, with all of the many small islands, would be the source of countless stories, just waiting for me to write them down.

Back in Graytown, Nick, Meg, and I all eagerly tackled the arduous task of packing. We carefully boxed the items we wished to take with us, but left the couch and other items we didn't want, to see if a new owner would be interested in keeping any of them.

The "haunted" kitchen table and chairs wouldn't be coming, but I didn't want to leave them in the house or even give them away. I wanted to make sure they were completely destroyed.

Nick didn't argue with my decision. With a chainsaw in hand and his goggles on, Nick headed to the backyard to saw them up for a final trip to the local dump. I sat in a blue pop-up chair in the yard and quietly watched from a distance. I didn't speak a single word, but a few tears trickled down my cheeks and dried on my face.

When he finished with the table, he stopped the chainsaw and moved the first chair into position for destruction. I stood up and called out to him. "Hold up there. Can I have a go?"

"Sure, baby, here are the goggles. Please try not cut off your leg or any other body parts." As I put on the goggles, he said, "Sorry, hon, they're a bit sweaty. It's more of a workout than you'd expect."

"Move aside, and I'll show you how it's done."

He laughed and stepped away. We were both silent as I worked to cut the chair up into as many small pieces as I could.

Satisfied with my own workmanship, I handed the chainsaw back to Nick and moved to sit back down in the blue chair. I silently watched him dismember the rest of the chairs.

When I was packing the items stored in the office desk drawers, I found a tarnished gold picture frame tucked away on the side of some of my original writings and notebooks. It was the five-by-seven picture of Hope in her white confirmation dress that I'd hidden from view shortly before her ghost first appeared.

I was about to wrap it and place it the box, when something Damian said to me in the hospital popped into my head. He had told me that he was a prisoner of your ghost. As I sat there and stared at the picture, I felt an overwhelming need to remove it from the frame.

I struggled to slide the backing out from the frame. Once the backing was finally off, I found myself looking at a piece of paper, carefully folded to fit behind the photograph in the frame. Inside of this folded paper was a small wallet-sized picture. I turned the picture over and gasped at a high school graduation picture of Elle. My hands shook as I opened the letter:

Dear Family of Gloria Minor Marksman,

I don't wish to upset anyone reading this letter. My name is Elle Sauder and my biological mother, Gloria Minor, gave me up for adoption when she was just a child herself. I respect this decision. On my eighteenth birthday, I reached out to the adoption agency to find information on my parents. They informed me that over the years, she'd updated her contact information in case I decided to reach out. When they looked up her social security number, they discovered she'd died a few years ago. They looked up the last address on file and it matched what I'd found in the white pages. When I read her obituary, I learned of a sister, Hope, who'd died a few years prior to our mother. Our mother died on what was my sixteenth birthday. To read of both deaths broke my heart in two.

Her husband was listed as Damian Marksman, and I'm writing to ask if it's possible to connect with family members and learn more about my mother and family heritage. Mr. Marksman, I appreciate if this letter is given to someone who can help. There wasn't a record of my biological father, so I'm not sure if I'll ever know his identity. Once again, I hope this letter doesn't upset Mr. Marksman or anyone else reading it, and please know that I don't harbor any ill feelings. I've attached a photo of myself, too.

Please write me back to my private PO Box 333, Boxington, NY and let me know if you or any other family members would be willing to speak and or meet with me.

Warmest regards,
Elle Sauder

The truth of how Damian would have reacted to Gloria's suicide letter had he read it years ago was staring at me. There was no question in my mind that Damian had known Elle was his biological daughter, the very second he viewed this picture. It was painfully obvious that he'd hidden the letter away behind this picture and hadn't written Elle back. He had made a conscious decision not to leave anything to Elle in his estate and leave everything to me.

With the picture still in hand, I sat down on the floor and gasped for air as I thought of poor Elle, who had figured out her biological mother had died on her sixteenth birthday. I'm sure Elle realized it wasn't a coincidence, and I began imagining what thoughts swirled around in her mind when she'd read the date.

I was sure that Damian never followed news of Elle, and died not knowing of her current circumstance. Hope's ghost probably began to haunt him shortly after he hid this letter and Elle's graduation photo behind Hope's confirmation picture.

The words of Aristotle echoed in my mind: "The soul never thinks without an image."

The Roots of Hope

Protected by the brown, tough leather-like shell
In a cup-shaped holder upside down bell
Defining odds, two seeded oak nuts reside
Until a white Keds sneaker double-knotted tied
Cracks the slumbering womb apart
And Nature's law of survival starts
As a squirrel scatters one seed which will thrive
And bring the next generation of the oak tree alive
Rooted deep beneath the earth, by Hope's wistful love
Watered by God's merciful tears from above

Chapter IX

Our real estate agent, Linda, called and asked to meet with us regarding the sale of our house.

I looked around the hotel suite we'd been calling home since we moved out of the house on Graze Street to make way for the open houses. We were supposed to be in our new home in Meredith, NH, by now, but there had been some delays in the renovations. That, combined with the offer on our house that had fallen through, had us living in this tiny space.

Even in our temporary quarters, though, I felt renewed. I had all the resources I needed to help me heal, both emotionally and spiritually, and my battle between free will and fate finally made sense to me. My therapy sessions, Bible study, renewed faith, and my study of the law of attraction had opened me up to the idea that I wasn't just moving as a chess piece through my life.

God gave us free will to choose to connect to Him or not to connect to Him. Once connected to Him, He could turn negative circumstances into positive. As the Bible shows us, He is able to transform "ashes to beauty," all in His perfect timing.

So, like Danny's sister, JoAnn, I no longer believed in coincidences.

As I tidied up the suite and made the queen-sized bed in our room, Nick came in and gave me a little kiss. "I've missed you and all the small, healthy things you used to do," he said. "Like making the bed."

I smiled and smoothed the spread over the pillows. "I'm back again," I said, "but I guess you can see that for yourself. A little more time will heal us."

"Yes, it will," he said.

A few minutes later, our real estate agent, Linda, was sitting in the chair by the window of out suite. "So, great news," she said. "I've found a buyer for your home, at the asking price."

"That's fantastic!" I said. "So what do you need from us?"

"Well, first there's something about the sale I need to discuss with you and your husband."

"Do I dare risk spoiling this moment and ask what that might be?" Nick asked.

Linda smiled. "I don't think we're talking about any kind of deal breakers. The buyers are simply interested in the appliances and some of the pieces of furniture in the house. They've prepared this list for you to review and decide what you're willing to part with." She handed me the list. "The buyers are also extremely interested in purchasing the boat in the yard." She motioned toward the paper in my hand. "They're making a very substantial offer for it."

Without looking down, I said, "The boat is not for sale."

"Honey, maybe it would be a good idea to sell the boat," said Nick. "She needs a lot of work before we can put her back in the water, and she's sat there in our yard for two years. We can buy a newer, smaller one for the lake. I know she's a magnificent boat, but she'd be more magnificent if she were used."

"Nick, I'm sorry. I know we always live by what's mine is yours and vice versa, and we've always been able to come to some sort of compromise on decisions like this. But I can't compromise on this. I bought the *Afta-U* with the money from my first novel. Not only does it have sentimental meaning for me, I think it'll help me heal and recover."

"Wouldn't a boat immediately ready to go in the water help?"

"You're right, she's too big for the lake. I was hoping that we could take a refresher sailing course and fix her up together. We can work on her in our new yard. Then, when she's ready, we can decide on a place to keep her – probably in Massachusetts, somewhere on the North Shore. Then we can take her out on the ocean, where she belongs."

Nick nodded and chuckled. "Well, I can see that I've already lost this battle, so count me in. Linda, the boat isn't for sale; it's headed for New Hampshire." He reached over and took my free hand. "I guess we'll just have to buy a smaller boat for the lake, since we can't live directly on the water and not have a boat at our dock."

I smiled. "Now why didn't I think of that?"

"Well, I know the Clifford family will be disappointed, but I'll let them know," Linda said.

I glanced down at the list. "Linda, we agree with the prices for the other things here. They are also welcome to whatever else is still in the house. Whatever they don't want they can donate or throw out."

"Don't you and your husband even want to discuss the prices?" Linda asked.

"My husband and I already discussed the items we left behind, and all these offers are just fine with us. To be honest, we agreed that just about any reasonable offer would be fine with us." I smiled as I thought about the washer and dryer we were leaving behind. They were both relatively new, but I'd already insisted that we purchase front-loading ones for our new home. I wanted to leave behind any of those missing socks that I was convinced the dryer had absorbed.

A week later, we met with the Cliffords and closed the sale of the house on Graze Street.

Summer had finally arrived, and so did the day we were to move the *Afta-U* to her new home in New Hampshire. I was filled with a new sense of hope, awakened to the possibilities of life beginning again.

I shouldn't have been surprised that the fog hadn't lifted that morning. It was odd how the fog always seemed to linger over the house on Graze Street. I'd lived for years as a recluse in that house, along with your ghost and the specter of unbearable pain that had shrouded it like the fog.

I prayed that this new family could find a different experience.

The night before our move, Nick had a few friends over to help him disassemble the wooden A-frame structure he had built over the *Afta-U*, then move the boat off the metal blocks and onto the trailer. When we showed up this morning, all we had to do was hook her up and tow her away to our new home.

While Nick and I were making the final preparations on the boat, the Cliffords arrived to drop off some boxes and take measurements in the house. I'd just finished pulling out all of the life preservers to put them in the back of the Ford F-250 truck for travel.

The Clifford's young daughter ran over to where I stood. "Hello," she said. "I'm Lilly. What are you doing?"

"I'm happy to meet you, Lilly. I'm just packing things from the boat so they won't tumble around once we're on the road."

"I'm five. I drew a picture of our new house. Want to see it?" Without waiting for an answer, she handed me her picture.

"It's beautiful, Lilly! Just beautiful," I said.

"Mommy will put it on the refrigerator, where everybody will see it."

"It will make the kitchen look wonderful."

"Thank you! I can make you one to take to your new house. That way you'll be able to remember what this one looked like!"

I smiled and said, "Well, that's kind of you, Lilly. Thank you."

Lilly ran to the car and took out all of her crayons and coloring books and strewed them over the yard and started to color a new picture.

Mrs. Clifford came out on the porch. "Lilly, sweetheart," she said, "why don't you take that inside and stop bothering Mrs. Rhodes."

I could see how happy Lilly was, lying there in the grass with her artwork, so I said, "Oh, Mrs. Clifford, Lilly's fine out here with us. We'll keep an eye on her for you."

"Okay then, thank you," said Mrs. Clifford. "Lilly, you behave." She smiled and went back into the house.

As Nick and I were hitching up the *Afta-U*, I felt as if someone was staring at me from the front bedroom window, your old childhood bedroom. I couldn't avoid looking up.

I'd never seen your ghostly figure outside of the kitchen, but I'd heard your voice throughout the house as my mental stability deteriorated. When I did look up, I was surprised to see you standing there in your white dress, staring at me from the front bedroom window.

I tried not to show any reaction, and Nick apparently didn't notice. He straightened up and walked to the back of the boat to double-check the tie-downs.

I turned away and saw Lilly staring up at the window. "Who's that?" she asked, pointing straight at you.

Could Lilly see you? I tried to control the shaking in my voice "There's nobody in the house except your parents."

"But..."

I could feel the blood flush from my face as I cut her off. "You probably saw the light hitting the curtains. Our eyes can play tricks on us sometimes."

"But you were looking up there."

"I was just saying goodbye to the house." I forced a smile.

Lilly looked from me to the window and back, then shrugged and went back to her artwork.

Nick came back and looked closely at me. "Is everything all right?" he asked.

I forced another smile. "Fine," I said. "I'm just a little bit tired. I'll catch a nap in the truck."

Nick looked at me for a few more seconds, then nodded and went to test the trailer lights.

Mrs. Clifford came back out onto the porch. "Lilly, please come in and help me. I'm sure Mr. and Mrs. Rhodes would like to get on their way."

"Okay, Mommy, just a few more touches. There!" Lilly carefully ripped the page off her pad and handed it to me.

"Very pretty, Lilly. Thank you, we'll treasure it."

Lilly grinned with pleasure. "Before you leave can I show you how the pictures look on the fridge?"

"Yes, of course. I'd love to see them."

"Follow me!" Lilly picked up her original picture and skipped toward the house.

As we reached the steps, I smiled at Mrs. Clifford and said, "If you don't mind, Lilly and I would like to see how great these pictures look on a refrigerator door."

Mrs. Clifford laughed. "Thank you for humoring her."

"Well, it may just end up to be the highlight of my day."

"I'm sure it will be. The fridge magnets are on the counter in a shoebox."

Lilly ran past me up the stairs and onto the porch, "Mommy, I'll show her!" She stopped and held the door open for me.

"I'm just going to go grab a few more things from the car if you don't mind watching Lilly for five more minutes, Mrs. Rhodes?"

"Of course I don't mind," I said, and followed Lilly into the house.

When we were in the den, Lilly grabbed my hand to escort me to the kitchen. She stood in front of the refrigerator and held the picture against the refrigerator, right at her eye level. "There?" she asked.

"Perfect! Let me grab a few of the magnets your mom said were in this box."

I took off the top of the shoebox and looked inside. My heart skipped a fast beat inside my chest as I found myself looking at a photograph almost identical to the one Nick and I had found on the bottom of the metal box hidden in the floorboards, along the documents revealing that Damian was Michael's biological father.

I pulled the photo out of the box and stared at it. There stood the pretty young woman wearing her brown skirt, long brown coat, and brown high heels, standing next to the smashed taillight on Damian Marksman's truck. In the original picture, the woman, whom I had assumed was Michael's mother, Marilyn, was covering her face with her hands. In this one, her hands dangled by her sides and she was smiling.

The woman in the photographs was clearly not Marilyn Grainger.

Lilly looked at the picture in my hand. "That's Grandma Clifford," she said.

"Your father's mother? She's lovely."

"My grandma. She was old, and when I was three, she left us to take care of Ralph in heaven. Don't tell my dad, but Ralph was a great dog, so I think Ralph is taking care of her."

I flipped the picture over and read the date on the back, this time it wasn't blacked out. It read: June 25, 1988. I tried to maintain my composure as my mind churned. That was not only the night before my family moved away from Graze Street, and the night of the town bonfire, but it also was Mrs. Marksman's first birthday after her suicide.

I turned the picture back over and looked at the broken taillight, the same one I'd noticed as we drove away and I waved goodbye to Mr. Marksman. There had to be a reason Damian had stored a similar picture away in that metal box. Peter Clifford's mother had obviously made an impact on Damian in some way or another. My stomach turned as I wondered if Peter Clifford could be yet another illegitimate son of Damian's.

I decided to leave that whole line of thinking alone.

"Did you find a magnet yet?" asked Lilly. "My arms are getting tired from holding up my drawing."

I dropped the photo on the counter and grabbed a few of the magnetic alphabet letters from the box. "There," I said, sticking magnets on the four corners of Lilly's picture. "It's just like an art museum."

I heard the door to the den open up. "Lilly," said Mrs. Clifford. "Come help me unpack this box."

"Coming!" said Lilly, bounding out of the room.

I looked down at the picture on the counter one last time, shook my head, and left the kitchen.

As I walked to where Nick was standing next to the truck, I took one last look at the large oak tree. It had a large red "X" spray painted across the trunk, a sign it was one of the trees the Clifford's had opted to remove now that the house belonged to them.

It amazed me how quickly change could happen. The Cliffords and the Crowleys next door in my childhood home had obviously decided to work together to thin out the trees on the properties, and I counted five more red "Xs" in the wooded area between the houses.

I turned back to the oak tree and walked over to it with Lilly's picture clutched in my hand. I couldn't help wonder if taking down that tree might finally bring peace to your uneasy ghost and break the spell on this house. I wondered if you were going to stay in the house as a spectral playmate for little Lilly, or if you had only come to that window to bid me farewell.

I stood in front of the old oak tree, taking in all the wrinkles in the bark and the freshly painted red X. I looked at the divots in the branch from the old tire swing, and for a moment I almost could feel that sensation of swinging, and spinning, and pushing off that massive trunk over and over again. I could almost hear our giggles, but I knew that these were purely in my memory.

I looked to the left and caught sight of a small sprout, a baby oak tree that I hadn't noticed before. I thought about new life starting where the life of this tree was about to end. I looked back at the branch that had held our swing and saw Tinkerbell, the ghost of my childhood parakeet, perched midway between the divots. She chirped at me, and then her image quietly faded away as a stream of light broke through the clouds and fog, highlighting the branch.

I turned and walked away, back toward the truck where Nick still waited for me. I trailed my hand softly along the hull of the *Afta-U* as I walked by. At the truck, I patted the stack of life preservers in the bed, now securely lashed under a blue tarp, and thought about grabbing one of them to hold on my lap as we left on our new adventure, something I could hang on to so I could just relax into my life and stop treading water.

"Ready to go?" asked Nick.

"Yes." I smiled up at him. "I was just making sure these wouldn't blow out all over the highway."

"Baby, remember," he said, "this is a new beginning for us. Happy thoughts only."

"Got it. No negative thoughts," I replied.

Before we could climb into the truck, Mr. and Mrs. Clifford came out to bid us good-bye. As I extended my hand to shake Peter Clifford's hand, I was struck by the familiarity of his features and the dark blue eyes that I had somehow overlooked in our earlier meetings. He was wearing a green colored shirt, yet, his eyes remained a deep color of blue. Those eyes were the eyes of Hope, Michael, Elle... and Damian.

So it was true: Damian had kept the picture and stored it in the metal box because he knew that he had another child, the product of a fling on his dead wife's birthday. My heart ached a bit, as I wondered if Damian was capable of feeling love, guilt, or even remorse. True to his character, he had cast this young woman and their son completely aside.

But maybe Damian really had loved Gloria. I could picture him smashing that red taillight out of anger and desperation.

Had God led the Cliffords to buy this house? What else would have led Peter Clifford to this place at this time? At our first meeting, Peter and his wife had told us that they'd never heard of, or even visited Graytown before beginning their house search. They were simply looking for a new beginning for the family to put down roots. If this was God's will playing out, maybe this was His way of providing Peter Clifford with a sort of connection to the biological father he would never have known.

Or maybe God was simply restoring the rightful heir to this house on Graze Street.

In any case, Peter Clifford had free will to discover and deal with his birthright. As I looked into those deep blue eyes, I found myself praying that you would move on, that you would not make this new stepbrother a prisoner, as you had Damian and me. I prayed that you were indeed simply coming to that window to say goodbye, and that you could now find peace.

Free will had released me from my imprisonment in that house and from my past. I was now connected to the light inside of me, and my new mantra was, "The past is the past, it can no longer hurt me. Live today in happiness."

I smiled at Peter Clifford and said, "Enjoy your new home," and released his hand.

It came as no surprise that as we drove down Graze Street with the *Afta-U* behind us, the fog began to clear. As I looked in the rear-view mirror, I could see the fog still hovering over the Clifford's new home, making it look like a hidden castle in the clouds.

We drove slowly through town, moving with the flow of traffic. As we passed by the Grey Lighthouse, it beckoned to me one last time. The clouds parted above it, and I could almost hear cheering in the light wind lifting off the water as we drove by. It was as if the unblinking eye of the Fresnel lens high in the tower knew I'd be leaving for good this time.

I picked up the binoculars I'd packed in the car and looked through them, directly into that eye watching over the bay. Dew streamed down the glass, and it reminded me of tears. I couldn't tell if they were tears of joy because I was finally leaving, or if they were tears of pain that I was leaving. I put the binoculars back in the case, and we rode out of town in silence. The clouds continued to dissipate as we rolled farther away from Graytown.

As we made our way up the road, I began to feel the sense of rebirth that summer brings. The sun shone through the few remaining clouds and brightened my mood as much as it did the sky.

At that moment, I realized that I was content with being in the here and now. I wasn't consumed by the past or worried about the future; I was simply experiencing the grandeur of today. I affirmed I would always take the time to enjoy the magnificence around me.

I assured myself that this winter, at the very least, I would take the time to marvel at the chickadees playing in snow-covered branches.

Beloved Blessings

The white *Afta-U* sails flying high and wide
Patiently waiting for God's breath to guide
This magnificent wooden vessel along
Maneuvered now by a harmonic song
Matched to the vibrational current flowing
With Manifestation at the wheel all-knowing
But freeing first all anchors buried deep
Leaving behind, dark blue waters that weep